TO SAVE A SOUL

A Novel
By
Nona King

TO SAVE A SOUL

This is a work of fiction. Names, characters, places, and events are products of the author's imagination or are used fictitiously. Any resemblance to actual persons, living or dead, locales or events is entirely coincidental.

To Save a Soul © 2008 by Nona King

All rights reserved, including the right to reproduce this book or portions thereof in any form.

ISBN-13: 978-1440480447

Production by CreateSpace.com, an Amazon Company
Typeset by Nona King
Printed in the United States of America

To my lyubimyj,
My love and my heart, without whom there would be no melody to my song, nor beginning to my story.

To my kidda,
The inspiration for so many wonderful characters. You pushed me forward with fun and laughter.

To my Lord,
My Author and my Muse. You understand my unending passion for the untold story and continue to bless me with the next tale.

One

"I said I wanted a drink!"

Para Sedi raised her emerald gaze from her mug to the rowdy group in the east corner of the tavern. "Trouble there, Munwar," she said under her breath.

The warrior to her right inclined his head, his blue eyes not shifting from their regard of his frothy ale. Instead, he adjusted his position to better reach the sheathed claymore on his back.

For the last week Para and Munwar had traveled the nation of Rommel seeking work. Unfortunately, a swordsman and ranger weren't in high demand, even with her knack for sleight of hand.

In all her twenty-one years she hadn't had such a challenge finding the next earned wage. *I need a different line of work,* she mused. Considering thus far her wages included bartending, bouncing and even merchant's guard or caravan cook, line of work wasn't the issue. This particular autumn no one needed an extra hand—at least not in Rommel.

"We should go before trouble blows this way." Para chucked a silver coin onto the table as she stood. "Shall we take a turn to see what's about town?"

Munwar glanced to the far corner and the mercenaries the tavern master attempted to soothe.

"It isn't our squabble, Mun." She swiped a felt cap from her short-cut red hair and then slapped her friend's shoulder, good-natured. "Come on. Up and out. The inn down the street a pace beckons and it promises me a mug."

Seeing their intent to vacate, the tavern master rushed to their table. "Is the drink not to your liking?" He darted a look to the quieted rabble-rousers.

"The drink was fine, Milord barkeep, what I had—"

A fracas ensued in the far corner, drawing their focus. "Those blasted— Please, friends, stay. There is a private room beyond that hall where you may take your meal."

"That's right kind, but we're new and need to take a turn around town to see where we can put our names in for a wage-hire." Para noticed Munwar's continued focus on the tussling men in the corner.

"Let me inquire for you, friends. You're travel weary. You take a meal and rest."

She tapped her cap against lips in quiet consideration. "A private room, you say?"

The tavern master nodded and turned to signal the barmaid to prepare the room.

"We'll take you up on that then." Para smacked Mun's shoulder to gather his attention. It shifted, just. "Come along, Milord Meek. We're in the private suite today."

Munwar gestured to the corner table. The tussling had quieted once again. "Would you like me to escort these men out?" he asked the tavern master.

"Leave it," Para hissed. "It isn't our squabble." Her friend had one flaw, that being a compulsive need to be helpful.

"No, no, sir," the tavern master assured.

As she feared, once Mun decided to take an action that ended any preceding line of thought. She blocked his path, a hand on the chest of his braided leather armor. "Mun, you're on your own in this one. You hear me? I'm tired, I'm cranky, and I want my ale. Until I get that, you're treading alone."

The warrior responded with a simple smile.

Para shrugged. "I've had my say. Now I'm off to my *private room* to eat, drink and be merry. Mayhap I'll be in a better mood to lend a hand after I'm refreshed."

"Fair enough." Then the warrior stepped past her without another word. He adjusted the sheath on his back with a simple shrug of his shoulders as he strode with purpose toward the tavern corner.

With a shake of her head, Para sauntered to the opposite corner. Mun was one of the best swordsmen she had met in her travels, that being one of the main reasons she chose to join up with him. But when it came to choosing when to get involved, Munwar Meek wasn't so talented. His habit was to help though a nice, healthy wage could have been worked out beforehand.

Para glanced toward the corner and hissed displeasure. The tavern master did his best to soothe the situation, though it was clearly beyond that point—Mun was surrounded.

It was a common situation for the warrior, and he never felt the least bit concerned. Of course, standing six foot, three inches and weighing well over two hundred fifty pounds may have contributed to that attitude.

Five men surrounded Mun, and these all dressed in the usual rough gear of a mercenary crew: worn leather and dilapidated chain mail. Unshaven, the aroma of old ale and horse dung was obvious even across the common room. In fact, a dark mood of trouble hung over the group as dank as their nasty scent.

It was the type of ruffian she preferred to contend with, if she had anything to do with them in the first place. There wasn't great risk to her person, especially not when Mun was determined to be of use. Of course, he was always single-minded in that regard.

She let out a fast breath and altered her course toward the group. Whether she regretted the action or not was beside the point. These men had put her in this mood, so why shouldn't they feel the punishment as a direct result? Taverns were for the weary, and the weary didn't appreciate being disturbed in the middle of a pint... or three.

The tension hanging over the group heightened, and she could read the tautness of action in their stance. Mun would find a fist thrown his direction very soon, which would start the brawl that wouldn't end without at least one cold bit of steel being pressed into someone's space.

Their life was nothing if not exciting!

The fist thrown caught nothing but air as Mun tilted aside. To the tavern master's misfortune, he took the fist to the side of the head. He staggered backward into a table, which overturned and sent the man heels-over-head over the other side.

The offender received a head in the face from Mun, the result of which collapsed the ruffian's nose and sent blood spattering over the entire group. To Para's surprise, the blood caused a complete shutdown of action. The mercenaries stared at Mun in shocked horror before lowering their gaze to their comrades' blood-speckled faces and clothes.

Mun shoved the ruffian with the now-broken nose sprawling into the group. "Another?" the warrior prompted. It amazed Para how intimidating he could be when he spoke in single-word sentences. Who needed eloquence when his expression and stance spoke volumes?

"We've but come for a drink," one of the group complained. "Why you be roughin' us up as if we're criminals? I'll call the lord's guard on you!"

"Aye, that so, Milord?" Para came to stand at Mun's side and swept the group with a jovial 'tread lightly' gaze. "It seems to me that you and yours have caused a bit of a ruckus for nigh on one hour. In fact, wasn't it your comrade here that sent him over his now-broken table?"

"That couldn't be helped," the man complained. "Your man ducked!"

"Ah. That puts it all to rights, of course."

The man growled and lunged, tripping over one of his fellow's boots to stagger into Mun's fist. Dazed, the man didn't cry out when the warrior grabbed a fistful of shirt and tossed him into a heap near the tavern master's inert body.

Once again, Mun focused on the dwindled group and asked, "Another?"

With a laugh, Para rested a leather-gloved hand on her friend's shoulder. "Let's give the men a chance to—"

A chance they decided to squander on a full onslaught against the pair. Much like a cornered animal, panic grabbed their body and thrust them into a situation that wouldn't end well. They made an admirable showing, but there wasn't much to do against a warrior of Mun's caliber. Finally, he grabbed a fistful of hair and ears and knocked their heads together like so many melons.

They yowled and folded, leaving Para room to dodge a jab-hook combination. She swiped the man's feet out from under him and he tumbled backwards to sprawl into the chair behind him. Growling, he dove forward again. In one graceful motion Para drew her rapier, side-stepped, and clubbed him over the head with the pommel.

He moaned and fell.

Sheathing her weapon, she grumbled as she helped the tavern master to his feet. "Are you well, Milord Barkeep?" She steadied him as he shook his head to fend off the fuzz. "That was quite the clock-and-tumble they gave you."

"Y-yes…."

Para sent a quick glance to the shocked barmaid standing in the hallway. "Miss, a hand?"

Gasping, she scurried to help the tavern master to his quarters at the back.

"No excitement here," Para complained, "and no relief for my irritation. I'm still a crank— and I need my ale!"

The warrior gathered two of the ruffians by their belts and lugged them out the front door and into the dusty streets. "See to your refreshment, Par. I'll put these away."

"Thank you, I think I will. If they've even kept it in their head to give me a pour."

Peeking down the hall, Para caught sight of a pint and pitcher on the table and sounded a shout of jubilation. Hurrying to the room, she just kept from tipping the pint in her excitement of snatching it to her mouth. She chugged it in its entirety and then slammed it down with a burst of "Ah!" followed by a less than feminine belch.

꒰∞꒱

"You know the name of this here burg?"

Mun sat at the dinner table in their private suite, leaning his scabbard against the chair beside him. He shook his head.

"We've finished a day and don't know what its blazed name is?"

"So it would seem."

"Bah." She straddled the chair, arms crossed against the back as she dumped the few remaining coins from her leather pouch to the table top. "Fifteen silvers, Mun. That's all we have to our name unless we can find a wage worth its salt. If it weren't for the tavern master giving us the use of this room, we would be sleeping in the stable."

Mun reached behind him to retrieve a black velvet pouch from under his armor and between his shoulder blades. He emptied its contents to mix with Para's. The treasure revealed a bluish stone, a token of some kind, and two silver coins.

Para's green eyes widened as she pointed at the stone. "Munwar, what is that?"

"Naught but a pebble found in the river a fortnight ago."

"A pebble?" Para snatched up his velvet pouch and the stone, spitting on the latter and using the pouch to clean it free of the grime. The stone twinkled in the moonlight. "Mun, this is a star sapphire! It would fetch a pretty price in the market square. Pretty enough to keep us living an easy jaunt for at least a year, if we played it right."

Mun accepted the gem back. He stared down at it for a long moment before offering it to her yet again. "You may sell it."

"Keep it. We'll sell it all right, but not until it's our last hope for survival." She took up the token, examining the front and back before giving the dull gold a bite. "What is this little bauble?"

"My charm."

"Luck?" Para handed the token to her friend, watching with interest as he rolled the coin with ease over the tops of his fingers. Then he flicked it into the air and caught it on the tip of his nose. "Nefa's ass! Do that again!"

Mun complied, but this time he flicked it from the tip of his nose, up over his head, and behind him to catch it with his hand. "Each morning and evening I do that. Keeps me alert."

"Let me see that."

Nodding, Mun flicked the coin to her with his thumb. She caught it and immediately began attempting a similar manipulation with her fingers. It took her several unsuccessful attempts before she was able to get the token to cooperate and travel along the backs of her fingers. "That is a good exercise," she acknowledged, tossing the coin back to him. "Mind if I make it my habit?"

"By all means." He tucked the token and silvers away, hesitating at the star sapphire. "Should I keep the gem?"

"You found the thing. Who would suspect a warrior the size of a mountain having anything like that anyway?" She motioned

Nona King | 11

toward the black velvet pouch. "Maybe we'll keep all our gems with you."

She hadn't much luck finding anything a bit like a gem of that quality, so she viewed it as a good luck piece of possibilities. Finding a star sapphire in a river bed? Yes, that was definite luck of the highest value.

Para tucked her coins away. "Maybe we'll walk along more river beds. What do you think?"

Mun chuckled.

A knock sounded at the door as he retrieved his sword from the scabbard and a whetstone from a leather pouch at his belt.

"Enter!" Para called.

The tavern master gingerly opened the door, peeking around to reveal a shiner that caused Para to wince. "Come in, Milord Barkeep." She motioned to the chair beside her. "Have a seat."

"Ah, thank you, no, friends. I have word of a wage."

"A wage, is it?" Para stood and ushered him further inside. "Come and tell us, Milord!"

"Oh dear, thank you, no, I don't need to sit."

Para once again straddled the chair. "So, let's have it. What news of the wage?"

"A messenger from Lord Pomeroy stopped by for a bit of ale and told me of his lord's request for help. He didn't offer much for information, I'm afraid, and said he will be returning to Pomeroy in the morning."

"Pomeroy." Para tapped the table-top, her brow furrowing as she watched the action. "Pomeroy.... Mun, have we heard of Pomeroy?"

"To the north."

"Ah! That's right. In Dengal, was it?"

Mun nodded.

"That's, what? Must be a fifteen-day hike; seven by horse?"

"The messenger said he could arrange for horses for those

adventurers that agree to the journey. I have but to go and tell him to expect you." The tavern master gestured behind him. "Should I tell him you're to travel with him in the morning?"

"What say you, Milord Meek? We don't know a whit about the wage but that a lord needs help, but... I say we journey and decide once we arrive whether it's worth our effort."

Mun tapped his chin with the pommel of his sword as he stared at the table top. Para smirked. He was a deliberate man in any action taken. It amused her to no end, but mostly because she was well-versed in the jokes and tales of warriors who knew about as little as a cave mouse in regards to anything other than swordsmanship. Mun fulfilled many of the tales, but not all, as he was a fairly intelligent man about a great many things.

Finally, Mun lifted his gaze and offered a single nod.

"Done!" Para exclaimed, clapping Mun on the back the same moment she focused on the tavern master. "Tell your messenger that he will be accompanied by two: Ranger and warrior, if he needs the class. Feel free to confess our names as well: Para Sedi and Munwar Meek at your service."

The tavern master bowed as he backed toward the door. "Very good." Then he had gone, closing the door behind him and scuffling down the stairs to relay the message to aforementioned messenger.

"A lord, Mun! Think of the wage that could come of this task." Para's imagination swelled with images of gold and gems of even greater value than the star sapphire warming in Mun's velvet pouch. "If it wasn't for the fact I enjoy the adventure of travel, I could retire."

Smirking, Mun readied his whetstone and began his daily task of sharpening his claymore.

Para tapped the table, gathering the warrior's attention from the sharpening of his sword. "What in blazes made you take up the clay instead of something more practical? A bastard or long sword is the thing nowadays. No one uses the claymore anymore, do they?"

"It was my father's," he said simply.

"Well, that certainly accounts for the runes on the blade. Was he a soldier in the lord's guard?"

"He was an arcanist."

"What? He owned himself a claymore?" Para wrinkled her nose. "Arcanists don't wield swords if they want to survive a moment's battle. The sword is for men, like you."

"He was a fighter beforehand."

Para scoffed. "Why would he become an arcanist if he was already training to be a fighter?"

Mun shook his head. "No. You misunderstand. He learned to be a fighter from his father, the local constable, but he wasn't a true apprentice. He became an apprentice when he began his studies as an arcanist with the Guild in Carmaline. He had little skill with a sword, but it was the only way he could help his family at the time."

Para nodded along with the tale. "Merchant guard, more than likely. Not much skill needed for something like that, and it pays well if the merchant gets from point A to point B."

Mun nodded. "He was a fighter until thirteen, which is when he was able to become an apprentice with the Guild, though they almost didn't accept him, saying he was too old."

"Bah. If he has skill as an arcanist they should take any and all that approach them!"

"He had natural talent, which helped them overlook his age. His limited skill with the blade also led them to accept him."

"Hoping to have the first sword-wielding arcanist in their midst?" Para scoffed. "How did that work out for him?"

"At his first battle he very nearly lost his foot when he tripped over a stone and dropped his weapon." Mun hefted the blade to show a scar on the hilt.

She restrained the laughter, nodding with somewhat feigned interest as she pointed at the mark in the wrapped leather. Imagining Munwar Meek's father as a clumsy fighter turned arcanist was a chore considering the man's innate talent. His grace in battle was unmatched.

"What made you decide to train as a fighter if your father was an arcanist?"

"I didn't take to books."

"Ah. Well, good for you. There are too many robe-wearing flame throwers around, if you ask me, and not enough fighters who can actually hold their own in anything but a controlled fracas." She stood to her feet and gave a stretch. "I'm done for the day, Mun. I'll see you in the morning."

Mun nodded as he continued the duty of sharpening the blade, inspecting the edge for long moments at a time.

She kicked off her soft-soled boots and crawled up onto the massive feather-down bed, wrapping herself in her emerald-green cloak and drifting to sleep.

Two

Para scowled at the tavern master. "What do you mean by 'he's gone?'?"

The man wrung his hands as he shifted his gaze from Munwar to Para and back again. "I let the messenger know you planned to travel with him. He said he had to away early. To make rounds to the other cities with his lord's message."

"Nefa himself doesn't roll out of bed as early as we have, and the messenger has been gone an hour already?"

Para scoffed. "What do you suggest, Milord Meek?" She focused again on the tavern master before Mun could form a response. "Did he at least arrange for some horses?"

"I took the liberty on that, friends. They are out front, though I've only just begun piecing together your supplies. I'm not a traveler, friends, so I'm afraid my list of items is rather small."

Para offered him a silver coin. "Thank you for your trouble, Milord, and the bed. We'll away with the horses and stop at the mercantile to pick up what you haven't packed. Can we trouble you for some bread and cheese as a breakfast?"

"Of course, of course." He scurried away to make it so.

"Sons of a—I guess we're on our own, Mun, although I'm not so certain I remember where Pomeroy is other than 'north.' We should stop at a town or three along the way and see if we can pick us up a map. I'm sure there must be at least one to be rustled up somewhere."

"We could ask the tavern master?"

"Indeed we could— By the gods I will! He must know something about it, and if not, we'll trip over that later."

The tavern master returned in a flurry with a canvas sack filled with two loaves of warm bread and a wheel of cheese. "I hope this is to your liking, friends."

"Ah, Milord, it smells delightful. Thank you muchly." She gave the bag to Mun. "Now, have you the names of towns we might see along the way? Vielle is the first, isn't it? About a two-day?"

The tavern master nodded.

"Would you know who we can talk to about a map?"

"I've a friend who runs a mercantile there: *The Traveler's Query*. Arthur Pomrae is his name. It seems to me he hired a cartographer. Perhaps he knows of a map?"

"That's just the bit we need. What name shall we give him, Milord Barkeep?"

"Oh dear me! I am Les. Les Randalofson."

"That's a mouthful of something!" she laughed, Les joining with a nod and a "Dear me, yes!"

Para doffed her cap and offered the tavern master a bow. "Thanks again, Milord Les, for the use of your establishment. Milord Meek, let us be off."

They purchased the supplies still needed, making certain to have extra. Such was always the better suggestion in their combined experience venturing into the unknown—or even venturing into the known. People were funny creatures, and often did unexpected things.

The morning sky shone bright as Mun and Para set off for Vielle. Melancholy bit at her head, though, and a bright morning wasn't doing much to ebb it away. *Don't let it drive you to the doldrums,*

Par my lass, she chided. So she took to the task of distracting herself from reasoning out the possible causes.

Someone had told her once that if you thought too much about the sour side of things, they came to pass more often than naught.

The first day of travel passed without event, much to Para's surprise. She had figured, due to her state of dread, there to have been ghouls or some other sort waiting for a stray step. There wasn't so much as a wild dog set to bark and bite at them. That, in addition to docile horses and weather that was mild and beautiful, put Para into a foul mood.

Calm weather on an adventure was never welcome– at least, not for her. Of course, she was a superstitious lass when it came to many things: be it adventures, new horses, new houses, new castles, or even a new dog.

She had a curse breaker for almost everything.

Some of her curse-breaking rituals became pretty outrageous, if you asked an innocent bystander, but she would perform them regardless.

Although, now that she thought about it, she hadn't performed a ritual for at least a month or so. Nothing too extremely horrid had befallen the two, either, with the exception of their lack of a good wage, of course. But that was hardly a matter of life or death.

Para smirked. *Perhaps I'll keep forgetting those little curse-breakers until I really need them?*

As twilight approached, Mun found a site to his liking. While he set camp and secured the horses, Para took it upon herself to head into a nearby thicket and persuade a rabbit or wild boar to join them for dinner. While the boar would have been an honored guest, the best she could persuade was a pair of plump rabbits.

Just remember, Par, you're heading to a lord's castle. He'll have a wild boar or three you can gnaw to your heart's content. The delightful prospect invited her imagination to detect the aromas in her meal that night.

"What do you suppose it could be, Mun?" Para asked as she cleaned her iron cook plate with a fistful of grass. "What would cause a lord to scatter messengers so far from his own bit of home?"

"A personal matter."

"Aye, it could be at that, since he didn't feel it necessary to give the messengers much detail to pass along. Lord's have plenty of 'personal matters' to attend to, don't they?"

Mun smirked.

"We were last out Pomeroy's direction when? Must have been a year at least." She shook her head, tucking the plates away into the saddle bags. "These lords can be an interesting lot. Some can be trusted at their word; still others would give Nefa himself pause as to whether or not to believe a word that rolled off their tongue."

"Indeed," Mun said with a nod.

Para retrieved a pipe from her pocket and filled it from the pouch at her belt. After lighting it with a stick from the fire, she settled back against her horse's saddle to stare up at the night sky. "Do you have a bad feeling about it all?"

"About the journey?"

The stars twinkled down at her, the occasional bit of cloud blocking a section of stars from her sight. "The journey, the weather, the breakfast this morning...." She focused on him for a moment before shifting her gaze to a large reddish star overhead. "Just about anything at all."

"I found it odd the messenger could not wait for us this morning, but no 'bad feeling.' Do you?"

Para grumbled under her breath and brought an arm across her body at a sudden chill. "Maybe it's just a peck at the head, but it won't let me walk by without looking, and I don't know what I'm looking for!" She frowned. "It's got me in a mood."

"You're always in a mood."

"Hey," she objected, offering him the long-stemmed pipe. "I'm cautious."

He accepted a few pulls and passed it back. "And cranky."

"Yes, well, I never said that wasn't the truth. But that—aye, it isn't much different than being in a mood."

Mun smirked as he retrieved a polishing cloth for his sword from the pouch at his belt.

"All right." She tapped the grounds from her pipe and tucked it back into her pocket. "I will take second watch, if you don't mind. Wake me if something exciting happens."

Nothing exciting happened.

They packed up before dawn, waking to hot coffee and bread with cheese as they rousted their minds out of the mugginess of sleep. They both enjoyed the adventure of a new location each day, so the act of waking wasn't a challenge. In fact, some days they found themselves in at least three locations before the day drew to a close. All depended on whether or not they wanted to journey long, journey hard, or simply wander.

Today, Para decided to race.

"I'm telling you my mount is faster than yours, you son of a sod-dweller. Look at the length of those legs? You can see the glimmer of flight in his eyes, too. Why, he could be a direct descendent of Pegasus himself!"

Mun fixed her with his usual stoic expression of nonplussed disbelief before shifting his gaze heavenward.

"Look, Mun, you don't have to race if that's what makes you look to the gods for rescue. I'll just meet you at the first tavern I see. How's that for fairness? I'll even warm a seat for you!"

"And should you break your horse's leg?"

"Then I'll be cranky and sitting on a dead horse when you

finally catch up to me. Good thing your beast looks hefty enough to carry the both of us."

His stare blanked and Para grinned. "Par," he finally said, "if you want to arrive ahead so as to be free to get information, go. You don't need such exaggerated scenarios."

Statements of such insight always sent a shiver right down her spine to make her toes curl. "Aye, aye. I want to get there first so I can do my own information gathering. Having you along makes it difficult to move without attention."

He nodded and turned to mount the saddle.

"But I still want to race. I'm sure my horse is as fast as the wind."

Mun heaved a sigh as he pulled himself fully upright. "Very well. You start."

"Nefa's ass, Mun. If you just let me go on ahead, it isn't any kind of challenge and I'll be crankier than a red dragon at the end. You either let me go without the promise of a race, or you race me."

Mun met Para's glittering green gaze with one of calm and patience. "You sound like my sister. She's twelve."

Para blinked at him. "You have a sister? I've known you for three years and you never told me you had a sister."

"It didn't seem important."

"It's not. But you having a younger sib is a bit on the odd side."

Mun smirked. "I was hatched?"

"Hah! No, I'm not saying you're the egg of a dragon, or whatever. You seem an only, though I couldn't tell you why. Maybe I assume you're an only because I am. That's a bit of foolishness, isn't it?" She swiped her usual cap from her head and scratched at her scalp of short-cut red hair. "I need a bath. I smell worse than my horse." Pulling herself into her saddle, she sent Mun a wave. "I'll see you in town. Try and pick up a few star sapphires on your way in."

She kneed her mount forward.

☙❧

Welcome to Vielle, the faded sign read. Para had to squint to read it as she passed under. It wasn't a good omen, but of what it warned she wasn't quite certain. At first glance, it seemed small but wealthy, which didn't follow the drab state of the sign. It was an interesting bit of a conundrum that piqued her interest.

She dismounted and led her horse along behind as her gaze swept the populace and collection of structures a second time. The people seemed friendly, to each other, waving and smiling at those neighbors and friends they had likely known since childhood. To her they nodded in greeting, some with a smile, but overall the welcome was muted. She took this in stride, though, because it was a normal state of affairs for a travel-worn adventurer such as herself.

She tucked her felt cap into the belt of her breeches and scrubbed at her scalp. The action elicited a grimace. She hated feeling as if she wore more layers of grime than clothes.

A search of the immediate area revealed a public bathhouse and altered her course. On her way she noted the location of two taverns, a bank, two mercantile – one being *The Traveler's Query* – and an inn. *Bath, then information*, she decided.

An actual hot-water bath was a rare luxury that Para would have fought the god of death himself to experience. Of course, if it ended up costing more than the silvers in her pouch she would duck out the back so as to prevent being forced to meet him in person.

That was never a good time.

The bath felt delicious.

Tempted to stay for an additional hour, Para forced herself

from the tub and into her spare change of clothes. As it was, Mun had likely beaten her to *The Traveler's Query* and retrieved every bit of information he would need for the remaining journey to Pomeroy.

The only tidbits left to discover would most likely consist of myths and rumors about this treasure, that haunting, or that family sword stolen away by such-and-such a family thereby starting a feud of some renown.... It seemed as if the stories didn't vary all that much from hamlet to town to city.

"Your own fault for not liking the rub of grime between your cheeks," she muttered to herself.

She tapped all her pockets to check contents. Then she snatched up her scabbard and cap as she hurried out the door, tossing a coin at the girl with the apron as she passed.

Mun hitched his horse outside *The Traveler's Query* as Para exited the bathhouse. When he caught sight of her, he offered a wave and halted his step onto the raised walk. She returned his wave, slipping her cap over her damp hair before strapping her sword around her waist.

"Bathed?"

"Yes, leave it."

"Cranky."

"Always." She motioned into the mercantile. "After you, Milord Meek. I'm still on the disheveled side of things." The one down side to bathing was the difficulty it caused with dressing. Clothes delighted in sticking to that part of the body that was the most challenge to unstick. It was the curse of the bath, she was certain—

Para grimaced. "You smell fouler than the dead," she complained. Tossing him a silver coin, she motioned behind her to the bathhouse. "It's on me."

Mun stared down at the silver with his usual blank expression at anything out of the ordinary. "You want me to bathe?"

"Yes, right over there." She directed him, again, to the bathhouse.

His expression shifted to that of horror. "I am not going to bathe there," he objected, adamant. "It's a public house!"

"So? What of it?" She indicated his tall, muscular stature with a single motion of her hand. "You think no one's seen a body like yours before?"

His rugged cheeks flushed as he shoved the coin back into her hand. "I will bathe in my room at the inn. Where is it?"

"I haven't procured us a room yet," she grumbled. Her focus honed on the duty of tucking the coin back into her pouch rather than to see his stare of incredulity. She could see it clear enough in her imagination based on the lifting of the hairs on the back of her neck. "My mind has been preoccupied with putting together a strategy for what questions to ask of Milord Pomrae."

"You don't require strategy to ask for a map."

This was true enough to the point that Para knew she had slopped up quite a mess by bathing for an entire hour and a half. "All right, so I took a bath! A bath long enough to give a sea serpent the wrinkles, but at least I'm clean and not smelling like Death's Day warmed over in a swamp. Perhaps Milord Pomrae will answer my question about the map before he gets a whiff of you and keels over!" Para gave a quick nod as she crossed her arms.

Munwar's already granite countenance hardened. "I am not bathing in the public house," he said in a low tone. With that he stalked past her and beyond to the inn – *Gwendella's Guests*.

Para hissed a stream of expletives under her breath the same time she snatched the cap from her head and threw it at his retreating figure. It fell just short, landing with a plop in a puddle moments before being further humiliated by the wheel of a farmer's wagon. "Sons of a—" With hands on hips, she glowered at the cap, the wagon, the retreating figure of her warrior partner, and then the public bath house which could be held to blame for the entire fiasco.

She kicked at a raised floorboard of the walk before stepping down and retrieving her now soggy and horribly treated cap. "I just got this one last month, too," she mused as she wrung the puddle water from its felt softness. It had been her favorite thus far, and she wasn't one to think much of a simple cap.

Grumbling about warriors with odd sensitivities and not understanding about a girl's need to bathe, she made her way to the inn. No one paid her much heed as she entered, and she noticed that a maid escorted Mun upstairs.

She motioned after him. "I'll just follow them," she informed the young woman approaching her from the back of the inn.

"He's taking a private bath, so that would be 'no'. But if you're staying the night, I'll take seven silvers for each of you. I will, however, offer you a credit for his bath and accept twelve silvers for both."

"Twelve—" Para's lips formed a thin line as she eyed the beautiful innkeeper. "Too rich for my pouch, Milady. We'll look elsewhere."

"Dervia is just another half day's ride from Vielle. They could give you a place for shelter at nightfall unless, maybe, your friend would rather stay?"

As they were only there to get the map for their journey to Pomeroy, she didn't foresee them needing to take much longer than an hour – to allow Mun time to wash the filth from his bones. Besides that, the prospect of staying under this particular roof didn't settle well.

Para lifted a hand the same moment she stepped toward the common room. "Too rich, too rich, Milady. I'll wait here for my friend. Better yet...." She halted and turned toward the entrance. "I believe I'll take care of my business and come back. The beast will be awhile, I think." To Para's mild surprise, the innkeeper

26 | To Save a Soul

followed her onto the walkway just outside the entry doors.

"You are a thief," she said in a low voice.

That comment drew a sharp look, her green eyes narrowing. "Best not to throw accusations of that slight around; they may strike you back."

The young woman's blonde eyebrow arched. "You deny that? You wear the dagger hidden in your cuff and boot. You also have the scar on your right wrist, as those born to a thief."

"Bah!" Para only just prevented a rub of her wrist. "I am who I choose to be, Milady, and I don't wear that title. I am a ranger."

The woman regarded Para for a long moment before lifting her delicate chin in a nod. "Very well, lady ranger, I will leave you the title you choose. Come see me if you don't mind wearing a second. I am Mariah Greenwood." Then she turned and once more entered the inn.

Para glowered after her lithe form for a long moment before sounding a loud scoff and stepping off the walkway toward *The Traveler's Query*. No one could miss the business, as its name stood out in bold letters and did an admirable job of calling attention to itself. In the window stood a set of full plate armor and a large shield still waiting for its coat of arms.

"So you should have a map, they say," she mumbled as she regarded the simple business. "Let's hope you're worth my trouble."

Stepping inside the mercantile, she was accosted by the sweet and tangy aroma of some type of tea. She wrinkled her nose and closed the door behind her, allowing her gaze to perform its usual roaming to gather any necessary tidbits of information – be it other shoppers, proprietors, dangerous louts hanging about, or bits of supplies she might find useful later. This particular sweep of the eye only saw the proprietor, whom she assumed was Arthur, and what appeared to be a young blond-headed boy

Nona King | 27

sitting on a stool on one side of the counter.

"Welcome!" Arthur chimed as he came around the counter, arms raised. He was an interesting sort, with a balding head and only standing up to her armpit—and she stood about half a foot shorter than Mun. Though, if he hadn't such a wide girth to him, he wouldn't have seemed short.

"I was told you had a map to sell by the tavern master in the burg south of here."

"A map? A map? I have many maps," he agreed while attempting to lead her to the far corner.

"To Pomeroy?"

"Just so, just so," he said, nodding.

Para began to wonder if he would find a way of repeating each answer. "I'd like to see that one."

"Ah, yes, yes, just so." He scurried back to the counter and bent to make an awful racket while searching through a calamity of doors and cupboards.

She leaned against the counter, offering the boy a nod of greeting.

He grinned wider than Para would have thought possible for a small face such as his, and the twinkle of excitement in his green eyes made her dread rise a bit.

"A map to Pomeroy?" he asked in a bright voice. "Are you going there?"

"Ah… no. Just need the map to make certain I take the furthest route away from." She hated foolish questions.

The boy tilted his head as he regarded her—and broke out laughing. "You're funny," he accused, pointing. "I like you."

"For the love of—" She stood on tip-toes to peek over the counter at Arthur, who was now on hands and knees searching quite a ways back in the cupboards. "Map?" she prompted.

"Yes, yes, I'm looking. No… not just there…." There was a loud crash as Arthur hit the back of his head on the cupboard frame while pulling back. "Ow, ow, ow," he complained. Then he promptly ducked his head back into the same cupboard.

Para tapped her fingers on the counter while trying to keep from looking at the boy, as she felt certain it would encourage conversation.

"I could lead you there," he piped up, his exuberance causing him to almost jump up onto the counter. "If you take me along, I could show you the way!"

Her eyes darted to the boy. He stood on the stool, his hands pressed flat against the counter. "Your parents wouldn't have anything to say about traipsing around with strangers? My warrior friend might get hungry and decide to eat your leg."

The boy laughed again, this time also bouncing upon the stool so that Para felt certain it would topple him into a wall.

"Look—" Her hands shot out to steady the stool. "Will you sit down? I just want to buy a map. I can't pay a guide."

"You can! I'll lead you for... ten silver! You have ten silver."

"Even if I had ten silver I wouldn't pay you that much for doing what I can do myself—with a map!" she insisted to Arthur. He had momentarily ceased his search.

"Ah!" He startled back, retrieving a kerchief from his apron pocket to wipe his sweaty face. "I'm afraid I've misplaced it, oh dear oh dear."

"*Misplaced it!*" She clenched her jaw and fisted a hand to keep from leaping over the counter at him. Instead, she looked to the boy. "Two silver."

"Eight."

"Three," she countered, frowning.

The boy tapped his lips with a single finger. "Five."

"Oh all right! But I only give you two now, and the rest when we arrive." The boy scurried off the stool as he nodded his acceptance. She grabbed his arm. "Just how old are you?"

"Older than you!" he quipped cheerfully, sticking his tongue

Nona King | 29

out at her.

"I knew it, you're sylvan." She grimaced and released his arm. "But a deal is a deal. Here; two silvers. Don't make me regret this. What's your name?"

"Henry. Henry Sidgwick."

"Para. My warrior friend – who might have you for his snack – is Munwar. You better get any gear that's yours, because we're off to Dervia as soon as he's done bathing."

Henry sent her another excited nod before he scurried outside and around the corner of the mercantile. She shook her head and stepped out into the sunshine, fists on hips as she commiserated her fate of inviting a mischievous sylvan elf into their mix.

Three

"Traveling to Pomeroy through Dervia is like crapping sidewise, isn't it?"

Para's body halted mid-mount as she stared at Henry Sidgwick. Even Mun paused adjusting his saddle to stare at the sylvan. "What?" she asked.

"You said you're going to Dervia, but don't you want to go to Pomeroy?"

"Pomeroy, yes." Para sent Mun a questioning glance. He shrugged. "What's so wrong about traveling to the town of Dervia on our way to Pomeroy?"

Henry wrinkled his nose. "Dervia isn't a town. It's just a farmer colony. There's no inn or tavern, either. Only houses for stupid farmers."

Para leaned against her horse, her arms crossed as she regarded the elf. "You know a better way to Pomeroy than the road through Dervia?" Henry nodded and her gaze narrowed. "Is it extra?"

"Of course not! That's what you hired me for," he complained.

"Good answer." She pulled herself into the saddle. "Lead the way."

On their journey from Vielle, the weather grew as irritable

as Para. The overcast sky didn't seem to affect the bright outlook of the sylvan, however, and neither did the drizzle. But it wasn't a storm, and from what Henry said a storm would have served them better. Storms passed to make room for clear skies. The drizzles, on the other hand, could last for days while soaking a person from the inside out, mucking up any remaining optimism at the easy journey that far.

Para lost all positive outlooks gained from her bath.

Henry was a good guide, even if his cheer settled like warm ale on a hot day. He led them through the nearby forest in order to protect them from most of the drizzle, the comfort of the forest's canopy doing little to overpower a constant prickle on the back of her neck.

She shrugged her shoulders, much like a person would shift to adjust a bit of armor that didn't fit quite right. The prickle remained; in fact, it intensified to the point that she could no longer keep it to herself. With a slight hiss she gathered Munwar's attention as he rode a bit ahead of her. He reined his horse to walk beside her, his expression colored by curiosity.

"I'm not feeling aright," she told him, this confession accompanied by a darting glance of the surrounding forest.

Nodding, he adjusted the sheath on his shoulders with a slight shrug, unlocking the first portion of the sword to make it easier to draw and strike should they have unexpected company. For all intents and purposes, Henry appeared at ease, even so far as to break forth into a measure of a melody. The rhythmic dripping from the forest leaves even gave the impression of singing along with the elf's bit of music; uncanny, to say the least, and creepy enough to give Para a case of the shivers.

"Why do they always choose places of this sort to bother us?" she grumbled as an aside.

Mun shrugged, the action causing his sword to lift a fraction higher from his sheath.

"The horses will likely bolt, a dagger or two will be lost in the brush – and I'm down to only four! – and we'll be covered with ichor that will require another bath. You won't take one," she groused, "because that's the greatest sin of all time, and I can only afford a couple per week or else not have my pint of froth." Para swore as she adjusted one hand on the hilt of her rapier the same time she checked the position of the bow slung across her back.

"The last time we found a map to treasure," Mun reminded.

"I know, and that bit of adventuring was a gas, but my arm was in a sling for two weeks and now it aches whenever it snows."

"At least you—"

"Know when it will snow. Yes, I got that." She grimaced. "Can't we move to a nice desert? Some place that doesn't have that infernal white madness? You don't know how much it hurts, my arm that is."

"Sand mites," Mun reminded.

Para pressed her lips into a thin line. "You just had to say that, didn't you?"

He shrugged.

"All right, you win! Get me to a nice quiet place that has no desert and no winter, with pretty scenery, lots of adventure, and the occasional gem to drop in my path. That's not too much to ask for a girl, is it? I would even put up with some lord telling me what to do. Or a kind of job even! As long as I had a room of my own with a nice couch and maybe a pint of the froth each evening to go to bed with.... I could put up with that!" She smiled, her green eyes brightening. "You know, that sounds right delightful. Yes, I want that. "

With an adjustment to his leather gauntlets, Mun nodded. "Pleasant."

"Is that all? It sounds like this side of heaven, Milord Meek, and you right well know—"

"Will y'all be silent!"

Mun and Para both reined their horses to a sudden stop at the male command barked from the deeper portion of the forest above their heads. Neither of them had noticed when Henry stopped humming, and he and his small pony were now behind them staring up into the trees.

"And just who thinks they're important enough to be telling me to be quiet?" Para queried the trees.

A single man dropped from the lower limbs of an oak, followed almost immediately by four others. All were dressed in the usual garb of a brigand. "That'd be me," the first man said, and he showed a grin missing several teeth.

"I see. No one I know." She sent Mun an inquisitive glance, even though he continued to regard the brigand leader. "I don't believe I'm going to follow his order. What do you think? Too bold?"

The brigand leader guffawed. "You w'dnt be so bold, missy, if you done know'd what's waitin' if you don't gives me your coin. And that right quick."

"I have need of my coin," she huffed, frowning while doing her best to seem as pathetic as possible. With the brigand acting so daring, at least two archers must have hidden in the trees. They would be difficult to find without first becoming a target. Fighting swordsmen, even if unskilled, was always more difficult when under fire.

A water flask hurtled by Para's head into the face of the brigand leader and sent him sprawling. Then a flash illuminated the forest shadows and smoke billowed upward and around them. "Run!" squealed a voice behind them, followed by the staccato sounds of pony hooves and the bump as Henry's pony pushed by.

They urged their mounts into a gallop, bursting through the

smoke after two furlongs and following after the pony as arrows whistled in all directions.

"What in Nefa's fire was that?" Para asked, breathless.

"Don't ask questions!" Henry called over his shoulder. "They can still get you with those bows, you know." As if to prove his point, an arrow sang and thudded into the tree to her left as she galloped past.

The group didn't stop their quickened pace for quite a while, thinking it better to get closer to their destination rather than tempt the Fates with a premature rest for their horses. The hurried pace served well to put Para in a better mood, though how the little sylvan had the wherewithal to make some type of smoke bomb out of a water flask still perplexed her.

Henry Sidgwick proved to be quite the handy addition to their party.

They slowed to a sedate walk and Para pulled her mount even with Henry's. The elf didn't look at her, too intent on pulling a small wooden flute from the knapsack draped over his pony's withers.

"Henry," she prompted in a stern tone, drawing his attention, "what was that?"

"What was what?"

"The poof and smoke madness back there," she reminded, using her hands as a dramatic reminder.

Henry waved it aside with a scoff. "That wasn't anything, just a little elfish powder stuff. It works every time." He wrinkled his nose in disgust. "We get those dumb brigands all the time and they never leave anyone alone. They stole my favorite flute just last month!" he informed, wide-eyed. "I had to work all day and night to carve this one just the way I want it, and it still isn't like the other. My goodness was I mad!"

Para couldn't imagine Henry mad at anyone. "Sorry about your flute," she mumbled, urging her horse ahead. Mun followed.

"Something tells me this quicker way to Pomeroy isn't going to be a simple stroll through the forest."

"I had that same thought."

She gave a shrug. "I suppose the best way to have an adventure is to go all the way, right? Hill giants, hydras, maybe a dragon or three to get the ball rolling…."

"Par, don't tempt the Fates with snide remarks."

"It makes life more… interesting that way."

Mun sent her a dubious glance.

"All right. I'll watch my tongue, you old hag." She sent Mun a wink. He smirked. "I can't believe you don't want to try your hand at fighting a nice, little green dragon. Imagine the coin to come from that? To say nothing about the treasure if I tracked it back to its lair before your sword had words with the beast."

"Dragons are more trouble than they're worth."

Para blinked at him. "You've fought a dragon?"

"That's what I was doing before I found you."

Para thought back to the cavern where she had first met the huge warrior three years before. "There was a dragon, too? I thought there was just that lich."

"No, there was a dragon also. They left each other alone, for the most part. I don't know why."

"So… did you fight the thing by yourself? There's a good time!"

"Of course not."

Para waited for more, leaning so far to the side that she tempted a tumble from her saddle. "What happened?"

"There were four of us: myself, Eveniah the cleric, Orion the arcanist, and Drew."

"What was he?"

"I don't know. He was never much use."

Laughing, Para motioned for him to continue.

"It was a long battle. When I woke, the beast was slain and

I was alone."

Para's jaw went slack. "Your group left you for dead? That cleric should be burnt at the stake!"

"Her talents were elsewhere. She preferred to beat the enemy over the head with her mace rather than tend to injuries of the group. I asked her of this at one point in time and she informed me that healing took too much concentration."

Scoffing, Para made a mental note to check the references of any cleric that wanted to join their party. The last thing she needed was a battle hungry cleric getting in her way.

Then there begged the question of whether or not they could still be considered a cleric if all they wanted to do was beat people over the head. Passion for their beliefs was one thing, but beating their followers into submission was another one altogether. *Sounds a bit on the evil side, if you ask me,* she mused. Of course, there was an evil side to anyone, more or less. Even she had been accused of being more evil than good. She scowled and adjusted her hold on the reins of her horse.

"I can go back and fetch one."

Para focused on the warrior, her face twisted in confusion. "You what?"

Mun motioned behind him. "The brigands. If you need, I can go back and fetch one here."

"Why would I want you to do that?"

The warrior motioned to her. "Your expression warns of building rage. I would rather you beat on a villain than take it out on Henry."

"Hah! Mun, you always know what to say to make a girl feel special." This time the warrior frowned. "It was a compliment! Why do you always do that? I give you a compliment and your face gets as hard as a stream of rocks."

"I have a hard face," he said, looking away.

"You know, I think that is exactly what I said the first time I saw your face. Remember? I found the way out of that cave."

Mun's gaze snapped to meet hers. "I carried your unconscious body up the side of a mountain and pushed you outside the cavern's small opening."

"Ah, but I was the one that found the trap that revealed the way out. This means, also, that I saved your life."

He stared at her with a blank expression for a long moment before one side of his lips twitched upward. "That is one way of looking at it, I suppose."

"That's the only way I choose to look at it. My ego is a fragile thing."

He scoffed. "Par, a dragon could beat you at a mind game and you would still believe that you are the more intelligent of the two."

"Why you— I wouldn't."

"Just like you wouldn't try to open the trap in the cavern that nearly killed us both?"

Frowning, Para's gaze darted away. "I thought I had seen that one before. I bet you a gold piece that I would have cracked it if that... that mouse hadn't ... erm..."

"Kicked up that bit of dust?" Mun offered.

Para laughed. "Oh shut it! So I should have left the trap alone like I said I would. So damn me."

"You do a good job of damning yourself."

That sent her into a fit of laughter which almost toppled her from the saddle. Only then did she notice Henry on his pony grinning up at her with twinkling hazel eyes. "What?"

"You're funny," he observed for the second time.

She frowned. "Henry, not all people enjoy the thought of being 'funny', to say nothing of having the talent of amusing a sylvan."

"There's nothing wrong with being funny!"

"I'm a ranger. Everyone believes we're dark and mysterious,

so having you point and laugh and tell everyone 'you're funny' isn't the best for my reputation."

Henry's eyes widened. "Oh."

"How about you keep that our little secret? You like secrets, right?"

He nodded, and it struck her as odd at how much he acted like a kid though he was older by about ten years at least. *Those are the elf people for you.* She hadn't had a lot of experience with them. What little she did… well, she always hesitated to trifle with them, other than a momentary meeting of course. It was hard to trust someone who lived so long. They knew flocks of secrets….

"Hey, Henry, you want to play a game?" Para ignored Mun's furrowed brow as she pulled a deck of cards from the inside pocket of her vest.

Four

Para waved to the retreating figure of Henry Sidgwick. Her smile served a striking opposite to Mun's frowning countenance. "Can you believe that little shrub had that much coin? I don't feel so bad about not getting a secret."

"Did you leave him any silver?"

"Psh." Para sent Mun an irritated glance. "I didn't fleece him, if that's what you're asking in such a delicate fashion. I made certain I took only enough to keep us in froth and bedding for a week. All right?"

Mun's ears reddened, but his glower remained. "My apologies. I—"

"You told me 'no' and you don't like being ignored. That and you don't trust me—why in Nefa's fire is it so blasted cold all at once?" She rubbed at an ache in her arm as she shifted her dark glare to the clouds looming above. "With the way the air is hitting at my face, I would hazard a wage that snow is coming."

"We should make for an inn."

Para nodded and pulled herself back into the saddle, sending another glance in the direction of Henry Sidgwick. He, however, had already disappeared into the forest. "Funny little shrub," she muttered under her breath.

As they made their way forward to the city of Pomeroy, she

paid more attention to the foreboding that had migrated from the back of her head to her front right temple. She took a pinch of herbs from the pouch at her belt and tucked it into her cheek, cringing at the initial bitterness before the spicy coolness. It always dimmed her most tenacious aches and pains.

"Head ache?" Mun asked, his stony expression registering concern.

She waved it off, shifting her attention from pain to impressions of the city. Pomeroy was a massive hub of activity built behind a soaring wall. However, the wall didn't present a sense of unwelcome as the gates stood wide, almost beckoning people inside. They were unguarded as well, and that caused a double-take from Para on her way past.

When did a city the size of Pomeroy leave gates open and unguarded—"Do you smell that?" Para hissed. The aroma of roasting meat set her stomach to growling and her nose to seeking out the nearest inn. She smacked his arm with the back of her hand, gathering his attention. "Come on. Let's get some directions over a plate of whatever smells so good."

"Perhaps we should report first to the lord Pomeroy?"

"You think he might offer a plate of meat? My mouth won't stop watering, and I think my stomach is becoming a dragon."

Mun smirked. "I'm sure a lord will have a plate of meat for two travelers."

"All right, let's…" Para grabbed the arm of a boy doing his best to skirt the pair. "Say, where is Lord Pomeroy's house?"

To Para's displeasure the boy directed them to a mansion that gave her a case of the shivers. "For the love of…. Milord Meek, why are the creepy places those places we seem to wander to the most?"

"A law of nature?"

"I don't doubt it." She shrugged. "Well, I guess we should get to it before I change my mind and venture elsewhere."

"There's treasure to be had here, Par. You wouldn't leave that behind."

"If my skin is in danger I might."

"That isn't what I saw in the cavern."

"I was younger then."

Mun chuckled.

Gesturing toward the mansion, the two made their way through the hustle and bustle with some modicum of difficulty. "What do you suppose has everyone in a lather around this place?"

The warrior indicated a sign in the process of being raised.

"Founder's Day, eh? Haven't been in a place long enough to see about one of those, have we?"

"Not as of yet, no."

"We might need to take a turn around to see what's what before we dive into the wage. That meat dish beckons my name with fervor!"

"I agree."

Mun stepped up the granite steps to the front porch of the mansion. Para hung back a pace, allowing the warrior the duty of knocking the brass ring in the lion's mouth. The massive door opened by a maid dressed in the usual drab gray dress with white apron and white mob cap.

She gave the pair a curtsy of greeting. "Your names?"

"I am Para, and this is Munwar. We got word from the tavern master—" She looked to Mun. "Where was it again?" He shrugged. "For the love of… Well, we heard that your lord Pomeroy is seeking some help."

"Indeed. Will you come this way please?"

"Lead on."

The maid directed them to a small salon just inside and to the left of the entry. "Wait here, please. I will fetch the master."

Para nodded with an absent motion, her eyes wide as her

gaze swept the room of unique artifacts and furnishings.

The maid retreated, closing the door behind her.

"Will you look at this, Mun? Do we even have these trees? They look too red." She gestured to the scallop-back couch of tapestry upholstery and a rich redwood. "I haven't even heard tell of furnishings like this! How in all that's holy did the lord get these pieces here? And from where, is what I would like to know! Can you imagine how much these would fetch—"

"Are you a city ranger, Par?" Mun asked in a low tone.

Para's attention snapped to the warrior. "That's not fair. I have an appreciation for pretty things."

"And the coin that goes with them."

"Hey. Watch that tone, Milord."

Mun crossed his arms over his chest of leather scale armor as a tall man entered the room. He was of a slender build with shoulder-length bluish gray hair and dressed in purple and gold. Though Para knew the Pomeroy house had wealth rather than noble standing, the quality of his apparel and his home declared the worth of a royal birthright.

"Welcome," he greeted in a somewhat bass voice, "I am Lazarus Pomeroy. You are here to help me?"

Para stood. "Yes, Milord. All we need know is what the bit of trouble is that you need help with. And what price the helping will fetch."

Lord Pomeroy regarded them both before motioning for them to sit. Munwar, of course, declined. Para complied, sitting in an overstuffed armchair with a smile as Lord Pomeroy sat opposite.

"My fifteen-year-old daughter, Alicia, was betrothed to Cyruss Kensington almost seven months ago. The Kensington family owns the palace north of here."

"Noble blood, are they?"

"Indeed, 'tis true. My daughter left to stay with the

Kensington family the month before the wedding. The morning of, the guards assigned to her protection were found outside her room, slain, with her body nowhere to be found. She is dead, I know," Lord Pomeroy admitted in a gruff tone, "and her spirit now haunts Kensington Palace."

Para sent Mun's stoic features a glance. These types of stories always put him on the path of no return. "What can we do for you, Milord Pomeroy?"

"I want my beloved Alicia to be freed from her haunting, but," he interjected with a single lifted finger, "but without the harm of turning or exorcism. Are either of you clerics? No? Excellent."

"You don't know how to free your daughter from the curse of non-life," Mun observed.

"Just so, and in the process of freeing her, I don't wish to sully the Kensington name. We have already been at war for so many generations…. Alicia was to be our peace, in her marriage to their first-born."

"First-born, you say?" Para asked.

"There is a brother: Derek. He is the local priest. He will answer any questions you may have of his brother and my Alicia's betrothal, if you feel you are up to the task."

"We're up to the task, Milord. In fact, we'll leave the talk of reward to after the duty is done." It would be nonsensical for her to decide a price if it didn't do justice to the effort.

Lord Pomeroy inclined his head. "In the meantime, I will give word to the proprietor of *The Journeyman's Palace* that your stay will be at my cost." He stood and accepted her offered hand. "Thank you, and you, sir. Please. Stay this evening for dinner and a bath. Ann will show you to your rooms." The maid appeared as if summoned by the mere thought of her.

Para nodded. "That's right generous, Milord, and I think I will take you up on your offer." In fact she had to keep herself from running up the main stairs ahead of the maid.

<hr />

The two were served their meal in a private dining room on the second floor in the east wing. If Para hadn't been a ranger, she very well could have become lost in all the twists and turns to their quarters. The fact did nothing less than make Para even more certain that her goal in life was to not only become proficient in wilderness tracking, but in having a mansion the size of the Pomeroy estate to heighten her rural tracking.

In fact, she found it amusing all the way through her bath to imagine the prospect.

Mun didn't care for the posh surroundings as Para did, and sat ramrod straight in the high-back chair as the maid took his plate to serve him dessert. The warrior didn't quite know what to make of the sweetness of the cream and fruit. It made Para realize that he must have been traveling in less than civilized situations for an even longer time than she had. That or he simply didn't hold enough appreciation for foods of the higher-class.

He retrieved the small silver spoon in his massive hand with some initial difficulty. Then, once he had it adjusted in his hold, he scooped a small bit of the sweet cream and fruit and tasted it as if the spoon would bite him should he take it wrong.

Her lips twitched upward. "So, what do you think, Mun?"

He didn't answer right away, so intent on the taste of the dessert and what he imagined it would do to his insides.

"Munwar."

This time he lifted his gaze to meet hers. "I think it's too sweet."

"I think you don't know when you have a good thing." Para reached out. "Here; let me have it. You can gnaw on the table."

Even as he passed her the bowl of dessert his thoughtful gaze remained. After traveling with him for three years, she knew what weighed on his mind because it weighed on her own as well—thoughts of the young woman and her tragic end.

Para lowered her gaze to the bowl of cream and fruit. She hadn't wanted to ask Lord Pomeroy about his daughter and what kind of person she was. That would have been a torture even after six months of grieving. *Better to ask the priest.* Everyone knew that people had a leaning toward talking about everything to a priest. Para doubted a fifteen-year-old nearing marriage would have been much different, even if it was the brother of her betrothed.

"You want to start tonight?" she asked without lifting her gaze.

That question drew his attention and a response. "That would not be wise. We need to plan."

Para nodded. "Talk to the priest. Talk to others that knew her and the families. It's not so late that we can't make a trip to the church—at least find out where it is so we can do it in the morning. I might head up to the palace for a look-see. It seems about a half-day's journey. I could camp out and leave the questioning of the priest to you."

"No," Mun said in his usual tone of firm calm, "we will stay together. There is something wrong in this place, and I don't think it wise to split up."

"I hear that, and don't have a thing to say against it. So," she set down her spoon and pushed the second bowl away, "what is the plan? I opt to speak to the priest this evening. Derek? Last service was just a bit ago, so the church should be empty."

"I agree. But let's not visit the palace until the morning."

Para hemmed and hawed on that request as she tapped the table with a solitary finger. "I would like to take a gander...."

"Evil things are out with the stars, Par, and venturing in without preparation isn't the way to solve a mystery."

"Right, right, right," she admitted, standing. "Well, let's head

Nona King | 47

on over to Priest Kensington and see what tales are to be told. Shall we, Milord Meek?"

There sounded a tap on the door that caused both Mun and Para to turn. It opened to reveal Ann, the maid. She stepped forward after a curtsy and offered a letter. "The master asked me to give that to you for Master Derek."

"Ah." Para accepted the letter, noting the wax seal and the crest pressed within. "His eyes only, eh? All right." She tucked the letter into her blouse. Before the girl could make a somewhat hasty retreat, Para reached out a hand.

The girl's attention returned. "Yes?"

"Are you off somewhere in a hurry?"

"I've duties, but nothing pressing."

Para motioned inside. "Do you have a moment or three to spare for us about the Miss?"

The maid's expression shifted to that of discomfiture, yet she nodded and entered. She accepted the offered chair at the table, sitting primly and a bit on the unapproachable side. It gave Para a moment's pause as the shut the door to their room.

"How long have you worked for the Pomeroys?"

"Almost nine years."

"You like it, do you?"

The maid nodded.

Para expected more information to follow. Servants tended to delight in offering details into the private lives of their masters. "And the Miss? Headstrong, was she?"

"Miss Alicia? Indeed not." The maid's attitude bristled. "The Miss was always a proper lady, especially after the death of her mother, poor dear."

The hair on the back of Para's neck stood at attention. "When was that?"

A return of the reluctance to answer caused the maid's gaze to shift. "The Miss was eight—just turned." Again, no embellishment followed.

"Was the missus sick a long time?"

The maid pursed her lips, irritation dancing in her hazel eyes. "The missus wasn't sick a day of her life," she responded curtly.

It was that abrupt end to the statement that made Para lean toward the girl swift enough to cause a start. "Look—what's your name?"

"Ann."

"Look, Ann. The more you can tell me without needing a rope and a prod, the better idea I get of how to help your master and the Miss."

Ann sent Mun a quick glance, the fact of which had one of Para's eyebrows twitching. "I don't take to gossip," she stated.

"Bah! Who's asking for gossip? Just tell me what you know and I'll take what I want from the tale. No one's asking for more than that, girl."

While Ann didn't look convinced, she did seem to relax her posture.

"Now about the missus…?"

"The Lady Pomeroy passed from the consumption after a visit to her sister in Carmaline."

"Did a doctor or cleric or such put a question over her death? Rule it foul play?"

Ann shook her head.

Para pursed her lips as she tapped a fingernail on the table. "And you say Miss Alicia did what now?"

"When?"

"After her mum passed. Miss Alicia took it well, did she?"

Ann's chin tilted in haughty defiance. "She was devastated but carried it with silent bravery. The poor dear. Such a lady she was; genteel and full of an angel's heart." The maid's voice caught and Para noted the tremble of her chin as she looked away. Then the girl cleared her throat and slowly stood. "If you'll excuse me?"

"Aye. Thank you."

Ann curtsied and left the room.

Para stared after her a moment before giving a slight shrug and focusing on Mun. "All right, let's get on over to the church. I've no idea where it is in this maze of a city, so we better get on out there and get some directions before everyone's gone to bed."

The two didn't require much in the way of effort to find the church, as the building had been erected only about 100 yards to the left of the Pomeroy mansion. It was a well-kept chapel with a somewhat large main room holding several rows of wooden pews, a stone podium and altar, and a heavy wooden door with iron hinges that led to what was likely the priest's chambers.

As Para and Mun entered, they noticed the usual tapestries on the walls, the crimson runner to the altar, and the crimson padded pews on each side. There was also wrought iron candelabrum along the walls and on each side of the wide aisle. While they chased away the darkness of the approaching night, they didn't keep back the chill of the approaching winter, much to Para's dismay. She absently rubbed at her arm.

Mun shrugged his shoulders and she heard the slight hiss and click of his claymore lifting from its sheath. She sent him a glance, her eyes darting toward the podium and the point of his intense focus. Munwar Meek didn't unsheathe his sword unless there was a possibility he would need it, and rather quick. Taking her lead from the experienced warrior, Para rested her hand on the pommel of her sword. As a ranger she didn't prefer tight spaces such as this because it rendered her bow useless. But a sword or dagger was a nice bit of fun, unless Mun got under foot.

Or she got under his.

Para frowned as she and Mun continued forward at a

deliberate pace. She found her fingers tightening their grip on the pommel of the sword as the back of her head began to throb. *Pomeroy would have given us a shout if the priest weren't to be trusted,* she soothed. But that didn't explain the current situation—

A tall man in the usual raiment of a priest exited through the back door. He halted at the sight of them. Para's frown didn't lessen. The man looked approximately thirty years of age with tousled brown hair and a beard and moustache needing a washing of the food remnants that dangled. Also, his priest robes were too short for his frame.

"What do you want?" he asked brusquely.

She sent a glance toward Mun, who continued to regard the priest. "We're looking for the priest. Drew."

The man looked to each one in turn. "I'm the priest."

"Ah-hah," Para acknowledged slowly, her gaze shifting behind him to the door standing ajar. The back of her head continued to throb. She motioned. "We need to talk with some privacy. You mind?"

The priest's gaze darted to the entry behind them. "I was on my way out to, ah, visit with a sickly girl in need of, ah, a healing. Come back later."

"Aye, about that… I don't think that is an option at the moment. Lord Pom told us to talk to you."

Again, the priest offered no correction to a misspoken name, which raised Para's hackles and adjusted her grip on the pommel.

"Fine. Wait here and we can talk when I return—"

The door behind the priest crashed open. "S-Stop him…," the bloodied man stammered. He leaned heavily against the door, his black hair matted and the blood dripping into his eyes.

Mun and Para moved as one, the warrior blocking the imposter's dash for the church's front entry. Para deflected his dagger as Mun grabbed the man's hand to yank his arm hard behind him. The man slipped free and bolted, Para and Mun on his heels.

The imposter grabbed at the door, crumpling when Para's dagger caught him on the back of his skull. Mun grabbed a fistful of priestly raiment and dragged him back into the church, slamming closed the doors to impede another attempt at escape.

"Got him?"

Mun nodded, adjusting his hold as he sought a leather thong from his pouch to tie the imposter's hands. Para took the opportunity to stride to the man still hanging on the door to his quarters. His face was a dangerous shade of white, and he groaned when she draped his hanging arm around her shoulders and helped him to the nearest pew.

He sat heavily as she made certain his head didn't smack against the stone wall. She dug into her pouch for a small vial, yanking the wax topper free with her teeth. Taking hold of his chin, she hissed, "Drink this, quickly," and tipped the vial into his open mouth.

He coughed but swallowed it all, unable to even open his eyes.

Para heard Mun come to stand behind her, his shadow falling over her and the man – whom she assumed to be the true priest. "Will he live?"

"I think so. Can you get some water and a clean rag? I need to clean this to see about stitching it closed." She pulled a runner from one of the side tables and used it to staunch the flow of blood. The man groaned. She rummaged in her larger belt pouch for her mending kit. "In all of Nefa's fire… who nearly kills a priest?" she grumbled. "Ah! Here it is."

Poking the needle into the outside flap of her pouch, she accepted the clean rag from Mun and dipped it into the bowl of water he set on the side-table. The task of cleaning the wound was slow going, punctuated by the pain-filled moans of the delirious priest. Once done, she set to the task of stitching the gash closed while hoping to have enough thread for the task.

After the stitches were tied off, she rinsed the rag and once again pressed it against the oozing wound. The priest's color seemed better. Para breathed a sigh of relief. Having the death of a priest on her conscience was not something she looked forward to.

"I think he'll make it," she assured Mun. When she noticed he didn't stand behind her, she darted a quick look around to find him kneeling in front of the altar. "I didn't know you were the praying sort, Mun."

He remained in that position for a moment more before standing and making his way to her. "Is it safe to move him?"

Para motioned behind her to the priest's quarters. "Aye, see if the bed is to rights."

Mun did as requested, returning a few moments later to help her ease the priest to his feet and guide him into the sparsely furnished quarters. They laid him back onto the bed, Para covering him with his single blanket as Mun took to the task of building a fire.

"I suppose this is a 'no' to getting information from Master Derek," she said, arms crossed.

Mun grunted his agreement.

"For the love of—" Turning, she exited the priest's quarters and strode toward the church's entry. The imposter had slumped to one side as he leaned back against the stone wall, his hands and feet tied behind his back. In all honesty, the man looked as if he were ready for the roasting spit.

She pulled a seat close and straddled it, staring down at the man with a narrowed gaze. He was just coming to. "I've a few words and questions for you, Priest That Isn't."

"Don't waste your breath." He spat.

"Oh, it won't be any waste of mine, that's for certain. You

Nona King | 53

might give a scream and holler, though."

The man glared at her, silent.

"Don't believe me, eh? That's too bad. You see, you've got information in that head of yours that I'm right curious to find out, especially with this attack on a priest. Who does that but someone who doesn't want that same priest to either: one, do something of use to another side or; two, confess some information that would make it right impossible for a bit of a plan to come about. What do you think? Am I right?"

The man spat, this time at her face. To his luck, the spittle flew wide.

"Now that wasn't a right choice by any stretch. Munwar!" she called, her eyes not leaving their scrutiny of the frowning Priest That Wasn't. "Milord! I've a problem here that I think you can help me with."

After a few moments of silence, Para could hear Mun's lumbering step from the direction of the priest's quarters. If Mun's initial appearance didn't impress the imposter, the first smack from the back of his hand would.

The imposter's gaze darted behind her.

Mun came to stand just behind her and, she was certain, struck his best intimidating posture. Para had seen it more than once in her journeys with him, the first being their run-in with a hill giant after their escape from the cavern. It was quite the sight to behold, as he seemed to grow and expand at least three inches.

She motioned a single finger toward the man. "I've asked a question to this Priest That Isn't and he refused to answer. Not only that bit of irritation, he up and spat in my face."

The imposter's frown wavered, his eyes darting yet again to the impressive stance of the warrior. Mun scowled at the man while adjusting the leather gauntlets on his massive hands.

"Now this is how the ball will roll," Para began, "I ask

a question and you offer me the answer without a lot of disgruntlement. Well, maybe there will be disgruntlement, but no refusal. How's that? Agreed? That way I keep my minion here from beating your face into the back of your head."

The Priest That Wasn't pulled at his bonds, the expression on his face a mixture of fear and anger. Still he offered no vocal response, and that began to pick at the back of Para's brain.

"Munwar, have a grip at the back of this man's neck to see if you can wring his brain loose. Or at least his mouth. It seems to be stuck closed."

In one long stride Mun was at the man, his large hand taking up the back of his neck as requested. The look of terror pushed aside any anger, but the man didn't even yell when Mun gave him a little shake.

Para swore. "Set him down. We won't get anything from him."

"A spell?" the warrior asked as he released the imposter. The man crumpled.

"Yes, a blasted spell. The minute I started questioning him, too. So not only are we dealing with a murderer, but now there's an arcanist thrown into the mix. How perfectly lovely." She pushed back from the chair, frowning, and tossed it aside. It clattered against a pew. "Adventure the hard way it is," she decreed, turning back toward the priest's quarters. "I'll take second watch, Milord Meek, if you don't mind."

Mun never did.

Five

Para checked the stitching of the priest's wound as Mun hauled the Priest That Wasn't to the local constable for questioning. She had instructed the warrior to stop by Lord Pomeroy's mansion and see about contracting the services of a local arcanist to lift the silence spell. Not knowing what he kept locked in his silent mind wouldn't hinder the solving of the mystery, but she didn't like secrets in general. This imposter must have a whopper to be worth the spelling.

She poured some heated water into the china basin beside the bed and emptied into it a pouch of white powder. After giving it a good stir with a clean rag, she used that to clean the gash. All the matted blood cleaned away to find a mountain of a lump on his forehead just beyond the hairline.

"You must have put up quite the struggle. Not so bad for a priest," she mused. Hopefully that same fortitude would trickle into his character type. That would help them solve the mystery of a young woman's disappearance. Of course, the fact that his brother happened to be one of the suspects might put a damper on things right off the cuff, but there was nothing she could do about that.

On the third rinse and dab the priest raised a hand to push away her touch, his eyes flickering open as he groaned. "W-Who are you?"

"The name is Para." She tossed the rag into the basin and sat back in the chair, her hands resting lightly on her knees. "Priest Derek?"

He groggily nodded as he forced himself into a seated position. A hand rose to his forehead as he winced. One eye opened a bit to regard her. "Did you stop him?"

"The Priest That Wasn't? Aye. Mun took him to the local constable. I had him head over to Lord Pomeroy to see about having an arcanist lift a certain spell that is keeping him quiet."

"There won't be anyone here that can do that." There came a soft white luminescence around his head and hand, and Para could hear the rumbling of a whispered prayer. Relief softened his expression. "Thank you for your help."

Para inclined her head. "Turnabout is fair."

"What is your meaning of that?" he asked as he gingerly felt the stitching. He winced again. "I haven't money for you or your friend."

"Money I can get. I need information." She pulled a linen bag from her leather belt pouch and dropped its contents into a glass of water. "Here, drink this. It will help with the ache in the head."

His brown eyes regarded the glass for a moment before he accepted it, draining it in but a few large swallows. He set the glass aside. "Thank you, again."

Para leaned back with crossed arms. "We've been hired by Lord Pomeroy to solve this mischief with Lady Alicia."

"I see." Priest Derek lowered his gaze to his clasped hands. "This is good. Too much time has already passed. I'm afraid…" He met her gaze. "What information do you need? How can I be of help?"

"Let's start with Alicia. What can you tell me about her?"

"Alicia is a sweet girl, generous to a fault, and well-liked by all.

She adores her father and would do anything for him."

"Like marry your brother?" The priest's jaw clenched, which caused Para's right eyebrow to twitch upward. "Some hard feelings between you?"

"My brother will always be my brother, but Lady Alicia should not have been asked to give such a sacrifice. Marriage? When she is still just a child herself?"

"Lord Pomeroy said something about trying to stop a feud."

Priest Derek threw off the blanket and shifted to hang his legs over the side of the bed. "No one remembers how it began, but neither family has been willing to make amends."

"You don't think they want the fighting to stop?"

"Lord Pomeroy may have wanted peace." Derek released a deep breath. "With a daughter such as Alicia...."

Para regarded the priest as he stared down at the floor between his feet. "Were you in love with the girl?" He looked to be in his mid-twenties, so having feelings for a 'sweet girl' would be easy enough.

The priest pushed himself to his feet. He was able to remain standing for almost a full minute before sitting with a somewhat controlled fall. "Alicia and I had become friends. She and I worked with the orphans, teaching them how to read and make a better life for themselves. During the winter she would work in the kitchens of the Pomeroy mansion, opening it up for those who didn't have their next meal. She would quilt blankets for those sleeping in the streets. Repair jackets and trousers for those who didn't have another pair...." Derek met Para's inquisitive green gaze with his own pained brown one. "She is as near an angel as we can be, Milady Para."

Para shifted in her chair, drawing her gaze away as she adjusted her crossed arms. "If she was such an angel, Milord Priest, who would have taken it upon themselves to send her to heaven? Someone who didn't want the marriage? Or someone who didn't want the peace to come with it?"

Derek raised his arms in a helpless gesture.

"Aye, there's the rub, and that is what Milord Pomeroy has hired us to find—the 'why's that no one wants to face. The answer to the question doesn't matter to us, much, and so it's better that we do the asking. That way the angelic Alicia Pomeroy can have her rest and the scum that murdered her can have his bit of justice." Para motioned toward the priest. "You're welcome to join us on this particular adventure. Who better to have along than a priest when the dead or dying are involved?" Besides, Para hoped that by having him there, the talk with the brother would be easier than she suspected it might be otherwise.

"I thank you."

"You should sleep a bit more, Milord Priest, to make certain your mind clears from that wallop."

He nodded and turned to push the blanket aside and tuck his legs under. "Are you going to see my brother, Milady?"

"It's Para, and no. Not just yet. I've a mind to talk to Lord Pomeroy about the intended, after you tell me your own bit of tale. Older brother?"

Derek nodded, his concentration focused on the task of straightening the hem of his blanket. "He is six years my senior, 32. He's a gruff man. Hard. Determined in all he undertakes. He has led many armies in battle. In fact, he led the army that bonded the four surrounding cities under the Kensington banner, freeing them from a feudal system that tore them apart. Father thought…."

"Who better to stop the feud between your families than an angel and a hero?"

With a flinch, Derek inclined his head. A hand lifted to press against his wound.

Para stood. "Get some sleep, Milord Priest. We'll be along to get you in the morning on our way to the palace." She pulled another vial from her belt pouch and offered it forward. "Drink this with another glass of water. It will help put you to rights in the morning."

He accepted the vial in her hand, bringing his other to grip hers before she could pull away. "Thank you, again, for what you have agreed to do, Milady Para. Miss Alicia deserves peace, and Lord Pomeroy deserves an answer to his question."

Cheeks flushed, she cleared her throat and gave a slight tug of her hand. Priest Derek released his hold. "Aye, aye, Milord Priest, we'll get the angel her peace or my name isn't Para Sedi."

༄

Para stared down into her pint of ale as she waited for Mun to return from his trip to the Pomeroy mansion. The chaos out and about due to the upcoming city wide holiday escalated. The Kensington family regulated the festival, and this year the Pomeroys planned on vacating the city for the Arielle Valley directly following the celebration.

Frowning, Para finished her pint and ordered another. Mun sat down heavily next to her, signaling the bar maid for a bit of refreshment. "Ah! Milord Meek, what have you heard from our lord Pomeroy?"

"He hasn't an arcanist with enough skill to lift the spell, but he sent messengers to inquire of the other cities."

"Nefa's fire...." Para's frown returned. "I doubt we'll receive a bit of help from them. They're under the Kensington banner."

"That presents a problem."

"Aye." They accepted their pints from the bar maid, a crinkling in Para's blouse grabbing her sudden focus. "What— for the love of...." Para retrieved the still sealed letter from inside her blouse. "It slipped my mind, what with the excitement of the Priest That Wasn't and everything that fell afterward. Bah." She tucked it back again. "I'll give it to him in the morning. He's resting."

"Is he well?"

"Well enough for the rapping he received. I think he'll be a great help for us on our way to the palace. I invited him along."

Mun blinked. "But he's a cleric."

Para waited for more. When it didn't come she arched an eyebrow. "That's why he's coming along. Is that to be the reason he's not to come?"

"Lord Pomeroy didn't want her turned or exorcised."

"Mun, Milord Priest doesn't want her wandering. If anyone will understand about Milady Alicia, I think it will be the priest. Perhaps he will know how to put her to rights?"

"That is true. Perhaps he will know the palace enough to help our search."

"I thought that bit of truth as well, although there seems to be a bit of roughage between the brothers. Not certain yet how to get it out into the open— Oh. What did Lord Pomeroy say of the intended? Did he like him? Trust him? Hate him?"

"Lord Pomeroy admitted that he didn't know Cyruss Kensington well enough to judge about his character. He had heard great things of his skill in battle, but of the man he knew little."

"Seems odd to betroth your only daughter to a stranger, and a man twice her age at that." Para gave a shiver. "I would run as fast as my legs could carry me before letting some nightmare take me as a bride."

Mun smirked.

"None of that, Milord Meek." She motioned to his yet untouched pint. "Drink up. We have a full day of adventuring in store for us tomorrow and a priest to keep alive at that."

"Does he have experience in battle?" he asked before taking a hefty sip.

"I didn't ask."

Mun stared at her.

"Why are you looking at me like that?"

"We are trying to solve a mystery involving murderers and many other things and you invite an untried priest into our party?" His expression was nonplussed as he splayed his hands out in front of him to enhance the question.

"How else is he going to get battle experience without experiencing a battle? Besides, I doubt there is going to be much challenge in that regard. The biggest problem will be solving the blasted riddle without starting a war all over again. My conscience couldn't take it."

"Humph."

"Why are you so grumpy? You've a pint in front of you, the promise of a full coin purse at the end of this bit of mystery solving, and you've already done a week's worth of good deeds by saving the hide of a young-ish priest."

He frowned at her. "You shouldn't be flippant when it comes to the dead."

"Flippant?" Para repeated, blinking. "When was I flippant?"

"Bringing an inexperienced priest into the house of death—"

"Bah! He's inexperienced in battle, Munwar, not as a priest doing priestly things. In fact, I saw him cast a spell on himself when he came conscious today, and a right good job he did, too."

"What spell?"

"How would I know that? I'm a ranger."

Mun actually scoffed, snatching up his pint with a slight slosh and gulping down a great portion of the drink before slamming the pint down again and ordering another.

"Keep drinking like that and you'll be crawling to your room." She crossed her arms. "I won't be able to manage you up those stairs."

Mun smirked. "So be it."

Para chuckled and slapped him on the back. "That's the spirit!"

※

Para tapped on the door of the priest's quarters before pushing it slowly open. She poked her head around the door to see Priest Derek sitting up reading a book. "I told you to sleep."

He looked up and smiled as he set the book aside. "I couldn't get my mind to quiet. Reading settles me."

She hefted the tray holding bread, cheese, and warm mead. "I brought a tray in case you woke during the night. If you're hungry now, you can have it with my compliments."

"Thank you, Milady Para. That's very kind."

"I told you. It's Para. Don't give me rank I don't want." She pushed the basin aside and lowered the tray, careful to prevent it from toppling. As she turned, she caught his scrutiny. "Something amiss?"

Priest Derek shook his head. "I only wondered…."

"Wondered what?"

"What made you seek us out here in Pomeroy?"

"Is that all?" Para straddled the chair. "A tavern master spoke of a lord needing help."

"You traveled such a way though you knew nothing about what would be needed?" he asked, incredulous.

"That's what adventure seekers do. The road is their home, and the next mystery is their song."

"That's very poetic."

She waved it aside with the same motion that she used to entreat him to eat. "Have you never been outside Pomeroy?"

"I journey to the surrounding cities, helping where I may, but the adventure is little, if any. The Kensington banner flies high, and trouble stays far distant."

"It appears someone sought trouble out this time," Para

mused.

Derek's expression fell as he stared at the cheese and knife in hand. "Yes. Indeed." He set the cheese and knife aside.

"Curse my tongue, Milord." Para stood. "Cast silence and I'll be out of your hair."

He reluctantly smiled as he met her gaze. "No need. The truth is the truth."

"Aye, but… well, never you mind what I spout forth. Mun says I spout like a broken dike and need to learn to plug it."

Derek chuckled.

"I'll see you in the morning. Rest as you can. You'll need your strength in the morning."

"Thank you again, Para."

Giving a slight nod she left the room, frowning as she strode from the church. The frown progressed to outward grumbling as she made her way to the inn and their complimentary rooms courtesy of Lord Pomeroy.

In her room – she didn't need to share with Mun when the tab was paid by someone else – she wrestled off her boots and stared at the thinning toes of her woolen socks. Then she tossed the remaining boot aside before crawling under the covers and snuggling deeper into the goose down mattress.

She stared at the wooden ceiling for a long moment before forcing her mind to slow its chaotic rambling. There was a lot to do in the morning to get to a place where they could solve the mystery of the murdered young woman, and she wouldn't be of any use if she was tired and snarling much like a red dragon.

Closing her eyes, she released a deep breath and struggled herself to sleep. Tomorrow would take care of itself. It always did. The best thing to do at the moment was to make certain she was ready for whatever tomorrow had in store. That meant she had to pay attention and be alert, focusing on her talent for sleight of hand while Mun focused on keeping the three alive.

She could only hope she hadn't made a deadly mistake in having the priest come along with them. Yes, who better to comfort the lost souls than a priest, especially one that had befriended the poor girl? But to bring a city priest into what was reputed to be a haunted mansion?

Para frowned, lacing her fingers behind her head as she pushed the thoughts away. The party would be fine; she had a good feeling about that… if feelings about such things could be trusted in the light of a near-full moon.

Six

Para stomped into her leather boot as a knock sounded at her door. "Come ahead!"

The door opened to Mun in full leather scale, his scabbard on his back and bulging pouches at his belt. The two had woken before dawn, allowing plenty of time to gather the needed supplies for their venture into the bowels of the Kensington palace.

"Just need to lace up this last and then we can go get the—" Priest Derek stepped out from behind the warrior. "Milord! I wasn't expecting you to be ready, truth be told."

Derek smiled; his brown eyes alight with anticipation. "I didn't want to risk being left behind."

Para stood and retrieved her scabbard from the bed. "That's the spirit!"

"He brought with him certain vials that will be of use," Mun informed, and he pat the pouches at his belt.

"Oh has he now? That's right kind, Milord Priest." She fastened the quiver on the side opposite her sword and then slung the bow across her back. "I think I've got all that needs to be got," she said as she pat each portion of her breaches and vest. She focused on the priest, noting the sturdy morning star dangling from his leather belt and the chain mail peeking from under his forest green tunic. "Impressive."

"My brother," was all he offered as an explanation.

"Aye, that would be the case, now wouldn't it? All right, then. Let's be off to what adventure awaits us on yonder hill."

"The palace lies within a half day's walk," Derek said as he stepped along behind them.

"I noted a direct path," Mun said, "but through the heart of the city."

Para grimaced. "Hold onto your purses, gentlemen. Five will get you ten there are scads of thieves trolling hoping for a loose purse or an open pocket. Stay on your toes and we might keep a fistful of our own coins in our pocket."

The trio did have a run-in with a thief who made the unfortunate decision of attempting to pick Para's pocket. She caught him in the act and threatened to take off said hand if she saw his face again, especially in relation to her own coin purse. The thief, a grungy individual older than Mun, whined and bellowed about the harassment of foreign travelers as he scampered off.

They continued on, the cobblestone under foot transitioning to dirt and grass as they neared Kensington Palace. By no stretch was it a castle such as what both Mun and Para had seen in their travels, but it still remained the dominant building in the city of Pomeroy. The path, as Mun said, was a direct route through the open gates and onto the flagstones at the foot of the massive front doors. These were unlocked.

Mun threw the doors wide and advanced with a cautious step. "It appears empty."

Para followed, but Priest Derek held back. "Bah! Thieves have been here and gone many times over."

"Thieves?" Derek entered the palace, then, his expression falling at the sight of toppled chairs and tables, and torn tapestries and rugs. "Why… why did father leave the entry unsecured?"

"Who's to say he did?" Para gave his shoulder a firm pat, drawing his gaze. "Buck up, Milord. Before this day is done you'll likely see a sight more troubling than this. Gird yourself for it and you'll be fine." She focused on Mun, who continued to regard their surroundings. "Come along, Munwar. Let's get to the adventure at hand."

The first rooms offered no clues regarding the Pomeroy girl. Nor did they hold anything of interest to Para on the side. Only one, what Derek identified as a resting room, piqued any curiosity at all. *"Why would they need a room for resting right by the door out?"* Para asked. *"Is the place so huge that they need to rest before trekking home?"* But neither Mun nor Derek could hazard a guess. For Derek, it was the way things were.

When the trio came upon Lord Kensington's study, Para's hair stood on end. In the fireplace at the far side of the room a fire blazed. Both Mun and Para began an examination of the room the moment they heard the first pop and crackle.

"A servant could still be living here," Derek offered.

"By the dance of the hairs on the back of my neck, I sincerely doubt that."

She made her way to the neat stack of firewood. The ash basin beside the wood basket was half full, yet the poker hanging from the mantle showed no sign of use. Her brows furrowed as Mun came to stand beside her.

Para took up the poker and examined the end. "Odd that," she mumbled.

"No fire dust."

"Aye." She regarded it a moment longer before investing another extended scrutiny of the room. Her gaze paused each time on a section of the wall on both the east and west sides of the room.

"What do you see?" Mun asked.

Derek made his way to Mun in curious silence as Para

stepped to the west wall. When she investigated the panels and joints with probing fingers, he whispered a question to Mun and received a quiet answer.

"Ah-hah!" she sang out. After inserting the poker tip into a nondescript portion of the wall, two joins separated to reveal a room beyond. She set the poker aside, turning to the men with a wide smile as she gestured them to enter. "Gentlemen, after you."

"How did you know that was there?" Derek asked with wide eyes.

"I didn't. I only knew to look in case it was. These rich types always have some sort of secret hiding somewhere. Why else do you think this place is so gargantuan? To hide all the nooks and crannies they have everywhere."

"This was the armory," Mun said, his voice muffled.

Para followed after him with an eager step. "The armory?" At the emptiness of the room, however, she frowned. "Look at this nonsense! Though I suppose we shouldn't write it off until we've had a look. My leather has seen better days, and it's about time you upgraded from that monstrosity you wear," she directed to Mun.

He sent her a slight frown but didn't offer a verbal discussion to the contrary.

"Ah-hah! I've already found you a replacement for your father's old clay." Para indicated a sword rack holding a broadsword, bastard sword, and long sword. She took up the long sword with a low whistle. "Nefa's bones this is a nice blade!" As if to prove her opinion, she unstrapped her rapier and sheath and substituted the long sword.

Mun glared at the remaining weaponry. "Par, these belong to the Kensingtons."

"Milord Meek," Derek said, drawing Mun's attention, "if any of this equipment will help you in your quest please accept it with my compliments."

The tautness of Mun's countenance lightened. "Thank you, Milord Priest."

"Like that field plate," Para said, pointing.

Mun scoffed. "I would rather take to battle in an arcanist's robe than field plate."

"Bah! You and your infatuation with leather armor! Fine." She motioned toward a display of studded leather. "At least that will give the offending invader a prick or two before he finds death. As for you, Milord Priest." She held up an earthy brown cloak sporting a brooch of common brass. "This I believe would do wonders to help in your protection. Unless I've lost a wit or three, an arcanist has cast a protection ward upon the thing."

Derek accepted it with a hesitant reach. "My father never confessed to something of this worth."

"Why should he even know what it is? Unless he is much of an adventure seeker, he wouldn't know an ensorcelled cloak from a hand-me-down—Mun," she scolded, "you choose one of those swords or, by Nefa's ass, I'll do the choosing."

"There is nothing wrong with my father's blade," he protested.

"I didn't say there was, you big ogre, and you can use it until it lies next to your body in the grave of your own digging. But at least take one of these others with you instead of leaving them here for those dogs to make off with in the night."

Mun grumbled under his breath as he took up the broadsword and shoved the sheath into his belt. Para gave a curt nod and then motioned to Derek and the cloak in his hands. "Put it on," she directed, "we've still a lot of house to cover."

"Are we here to plunder their estate?" Mun's complaint drew a sharp glare from Para. "You forget our intent."

"Milord—"

Mun interrupted the priest with a single, hawkish glance.

Nona King | 71

Para crossed her arms. "Munwar Meek, I don't appreciate that tone. I noticed a door in the resting room and game room both, and I would like to make certain there are no more secret doors or exits waiting to open with surprises of a less positive kind."

The warrior cast a dubious glance.

The group followed her back through the study and parlor to investigate the other side of the game room. An outside patio, Derek remembered it to be a resting place for those who had spent the day riding. On the other side was an inside patio for watching archery contests, sparring, and other hobbies of violence the nobility seemed to enjoy. Beyond was another game room, although this one measured twice again as large as the previous. Before the thieves had relieved it of its contents, Derek said it displayed trophies and equipment needed for the contests.

Para shook her head. "It would be better to have less palace and more outside adventure, Milord Priest."

Derek nodded in agreement.

"Not to give the Fates any ideas," Para said on their way back to the study, "but all this adventuring is on the boring side. Wasn't there to be a ghost in this 'haunted' palace?"

Mun hissed as he pushed through to the doors that led into the dining room.

"What? I told them not to get any ideas," she said, her tone pinched in irritation. "What more can a girl do?"

"Keep your tongue attached to your senses."

"Bah! If the powers that be can't stand a bit of fussing between friends, my hands are tied."

Mun sent a glance heavenward as Para shifted her focus to a scrutiny of the dining room.

Her frown vanished. "Hm. Table and chairs for a nice sized party. The bandits must have had quite a few before making off with the last bit of tapestry." She motioned Mun to the east and Derek to the west. "I'll take a look through these doors here, and you poke your head there. Give a shout if something flies at you."

Derek's expression shifted to one of reluctance but he complied, opening the door from the dining hall with cautious slowness. Para shook her head, amusement twinkling in her green eyes. Her assigned door led to a hall and the servants' sleeping quarters. Each one brought a sneer and grimace at the chaos behind their doors. When she reached the last on the right, however, the hairs on the nape of her neck stood on end with a tingle that raced to her toes. Each chair, bed, and article of clothing was tidy, clean and folded as if the person who slept there had only just finished their chores.

Para shivered, her fingers tightening their hold on the doorknob just as Derek shouted her name. She spun and strode down the hall, meeting Mun in the dining room. When the pair reached Derek's position, he stared at an adjoining door with a somewhat startled expression.

He met her inquisitive gaze. "I heard an odd noise."

"Not rats or mice?"

"No." His expression grew taut with thoughtful concentration. "It seemed more like the scuff of feet on steps suddenly silenced."

Para's eyes lit up. "Secret stairs leading to underworlds of adventure," she said in a hushed voice. "Mun, which should we explore first? There was a staircase in the hall just around the corner that I'm sure led upstairs."

"We should make certain the house is uninhabited before we venture down."

"My thoughts exactly. Don't want someone jumping us from behind, do we?"

"Should we split up?" Derek asked. "I can search the

upstairs."

"And if there are brigands in the closet? What do you propose then?"

"Much as you seem to think it, Milady Para, I'm not completely helpless. Yes, I'm a priest, and no, I haven't had the history of adventures as you yourself, but I'm the son of a feudal lord and the brother of one of our nation's heroes."

Para gripped his shoulder. "My apologies, Milord Priest, and you're right to scold. That said, I'm not fond of the idea of splitting the three of us, especially not when I have a case of the shivers that won't be soothed away. Something is lurking in one of these corners and I would rather not be by my lonesome when it deems to be found."

Derek chuckled. "You mean you would rather—"

"Never mind this, that, or the other. We aren't going on a solo adventure in a place like this and that is the end of the story." She looked to Mun for confirmation. He inclined his head. "All right. It's agreed. Now, shall we pull a coin and decide which we search next?" she asked as she pulled a coin from her pouch. "I'm all for leaving it to chance."

"I agree with you and Milord Munwar: We should search upstairs and make certain we are alone. The curiosity of the fire should be addressed, don't you think?"

Nodding, Para followed Mun from the kitchen, Derek falling into step beside her. "A good observation, Milord Priest, and when I show you the cleanliness of the room in the hall, that curiosity will be piqued all the higher."

"Clean? As if the person still resides in the room?"

"Aye." She opened the aforementioned bedroom door so both Mun and Derek could observe the state of tidiness. "All the others had the look of a sty for a herd of pigs. But isn't this last pristine? Yet have we seen a body at all? Has anyone greeted us, servant or master?" Para shook her head, Priest Derek nodding along with her questions.

"Quite the intriguing situation," he admitted as she closed the door yet again. "It certainly gives one pause to entertain the thought of ghosts."

"Or someone who is set against giving a 'hello' to a trio of adventure seekers such as ourselves. What is the world coming to?"

Derek chuckled. "You know better than many of us, Mila—"

"Tsk," she hissed, following Mun as he led the way up the second story stairs. "I thought we agreed not to ply me with titles. I'm a ranger, not a bit noble, and refuse to respond to another 'Milady' chucked my direction."

He raised his arms in defense, smiling. "My apologies. Habit?"

"Habits can be broken, or break the head of the one doing the deed." She winked. "Let's not have any head breaking between friends."

"Agreed."

Para gave a curt nod before focusing on Mun. "About what time have you, Milord Meek? We should decide if we're up to spending the night, or heading back to start Day Two on a note of peaceful slumber. Adventuring causes the clock to tumble around on the fast tick," she offered as an aside.

"If we opt to sleep here," Mun said, "we should make certain to have a room with an additional exit."

"Indeed," Para agreed. "So, let's take a gander what is up here and abouts, and perhaps we'll break for lunch before our stomachs rumble awake the dead."

"Shall we start at the far end and make our way back this way?"

"That would seem to make sense, since we're coming back this way for that secret door in the kitchen. What say you?" she asked Derek. "Any inkling of having better times one way versus the other?"

"I could offer a prayer regarding that," he told them, and knelt with folded hands before either Mun or Para could offer comment.

Para regarded him in curiosity, her hands resting on her hips as he offered his prayer and then waited for a response as if it were the most routine of activities. Unlike Mun, she hadn't many experiences with clerics or priests. Her initial impression wasn't negative, but she still had more questions than answers regarding their motivations. Being devoted to a deity as the sole motivation for one's life seemed on the odd side—at least to her. Neither did it seem very free. But she supposed that if they made the choice to follow that particular class, it was freedom enough for them. Would it be enough freedom for her? For Mun?

Like anything, it depended on life. There was many a thing in life that should have been easy and ended in gray because of 'it depends.' She would be the first to admit that. Life was one of the greatest influences in a person's future.

Derek lifted his head and met her scrutiny. "While I'm not so certain I understand, the god said there were many futures waiting."

Para grimaced. "Not good, but not like immediate death. Nefa's bones.... Well, I don't feel convinced one is better than the other, so let's keep it simple and just peek in each room as we get to the back there. Then we can take deeper looks on the return, if something tickles our eyes, that is."

None of the first rooms tickled their eyes or their fancy.

Like downstairs, thieves had made off with most everything of any interest, leaving the palace rooms in a type of muddled mayhem that made it difficult to comprehend what they saw. Even Derek began to grumble a complaint about people's disregard for the homes of others. Para felt a smattering of sympathy for the man, but she knew this experience would harden him in a way only life could. It would be a nice, healthy thickening to his skin that would ready him for a different kind of future as a priest, one that he would have the freedom of following or leaving aside.

At the second door on the left Para noticed that Mun's reach hesitated.

"What's got you by the craw, Milord? Want me to take a look?"

"Indeed."

Para retrieved a small leather cylinder from one of the pouches at her belt. Untying the leather thong to open the cap, she retrieved a collection of slender tools. She inserted two of these into the keyhole and closed one eye, the other shifting its gaze to the ceiling as her tongue flicked out to one side. Para never concerned herself with what Mun said about the gyrations her tongue performed while focused on her duty of unlocking or un-trapping. To her way of thinking, they prevented the two from having singed eyebrows and lost fingers at a sprung trap gone awry.

There was a soft click and Para hissed, "Gotcha," before tucking her tools away and slipping the hard leather case back into the pouch.

"Did you check for traps?" Mun asked.

"I did that before I sprung the lock." She winked at the warrior. "I learn from past mistakes, Milord Meek, believe it or not." As if to prove her point, she reached out and opened the door without a problem.

Mun smirked. "If you didn't clench your fist just as you turned the knob you would be more believable."

"Hah! I'll work on that." She motioned to Derek. "After you."

"Par."

"Ah. Amend that, Milord Priest." She stepped beside Mun, performing a cursory glance of the room with a narrowed gaze. Vials and beakers were smashed and broken throughout, many still holding liquid. On the far wall stood a shelf and rack holding ten unbroken vials. "Derek?"

The priest entered the room. "Yes?"

"Did your father have an arcanist on staff?"

Derek looked about the room with a curious glance. "Not that I knew of. The nearest arcanist's guild is at least a month's journey away."

Para absently nodded. She sent Mun a glance. "What do you think?"

"It's clearly an arcanist's realm. Experimentation?"

"Then there's no telling what we'll find on the other side of those walls there," she said, shivering as she pointed to the opposite walls.

"Indeed."

"Well...." Para rested fists on hips as she regarded the rack and the labeled vials. "Let's see what we can see and take what we can. Never know what will come in handy in a place like this."

Nodding, Mun made his way to the rack to slip five of the ten vials into his pouches after taking a moment to read each label.

Para shifted her gaze to Derek. "No idea?"

"None," he said, shaking his head. "Father never held much interest in the arcanist arts."

"Was he ill?" Again, Derek shook his head. Para frowned. "A secret that doesn't want to be told, eh? Hm. Maybe we'll be able to find something in his room that will do a little confessing."

To Para's irritation, the Kensington lord didn't have anything of interest in his room. Not even a single piece of paper that seemed out of the ordinary. The connecting library wasn't much better, holding such tripe as *Why Mages Are Better*, *Marvin, the Man*

78 | To Save a Soul

Behind the Mythos, and *Familiars Not Necessarily Familiar*. Para very nearly took the books with her to use for fodder for the next fireplace they discovered. Mun was able to persuade her to the contrary, but only because he said she would be the one to carry them. She didn't want to be bothered, so she left them behind.

Derek paused at a writing desk beside a bookcase, thumbing through the loose bits of paper with a thoughtful expression.

"What's got your mind wrapped?" Para asked as she came to stand beside him.

"I don't understand why the palace has been left in such a sad shape," he admitted. "It has only been six months since Alicia disappeared. This was to be their place of residence after the wedding, so why is it now in shambles?"

"Are you not so convinced it's just in the last few weeks?"

Derek pushed away the papers and turned away, his brown eyes scrutinizing the room. "Cyruss didn't approve Father's arrangement of marriage between him and Alicia Pomeroy."

"Oh really now?" Para dusted off a section of a table in the library and sat, interest twinkling in her green eyes. She hadn't felt the time appropriate to query him about the relationship of his brother with the Pomeroy family. Now she was comforted that the choice was a good one.

"Cyruss has been the independent militia officer since he was first purchased into the rank at the age of 16." Derek met Para's inquisitive gaze. "You must realize that my brother has been studying weaponry and fighting since he was six. That was always Father's plan for him: Battle. I, being the second born, was allowed to choose my path. Cyruss had it chosen for him and has walked that path loyally his entire life."

"Milord Priest, I know more than most about the responsibilities that life brings into play. Are you tallying something up to that life? An excuse?"

"No, not at all, mi—Para," he said, catching himself just in

Nona King | 79

time. "Perspective is needed in order to understand anyone and the path they walk, even should they be in the wrong. Understanding motivations often leads to a light shed on a repercussion or a solution."

She gave a single nod. "Well said." She sent Mun a sidelong glance. He stood at the entry to the room, keeping a keen eye out into the hall for any trespassers onto the trio's safety. "This life of independence caused him to, what? Refuse the match? Lord Pomeroy didn't mention a word of a 'no' that might have been said. Alicia made her way here in good faith of having some nuptials at the end of the journey."

"I know," Derek said, nodding, and his countenance tightened in an expression of perplexity. "This is what I don't understand. Cyruss communicated to me that he did not want the match. That he intended to refuse. That he had already communicated that to Father. I am not certain if he was determined to settle the feud himself, without the use of a tradition such as marriage, or if he did not appreciate being used much like a pawn."

"Would your brother murder a girl like Alicia?"

Seven

The question's only answer was silence for a long moment as Derek stared down at the bare floor. While Para couldn't commiserate the pain he felt, she could understand the complication with the situation. How did one investigate the murder of a friend when one's brother was the best suspect?

"It's a question to ponder," she said as she stood, "and that isn't to say I think you wouldn't be up to the thought before now. You're a wise one, Milord Priest, and you don't let little things like 'brother' this and 'family' that take you off the trek to the truth."

"The answer is beyond my comprehension at the moment," he admitted.

Para gave his shoulder a brief grip as she passed him. "We'll help you get the answer, Derek, and maybe it will be different than we think."

"That is my daily prayer, but my heart isn't in the seeking."

"Aye. There's the rub." Sending Mun a nod of acknowledgement that they were ready to move on, she gestured Derek forward. "Come along, Milord. We've another few rooms to peek into before we can get to the heart of the matter, and I've a feeling things will get a bit more interesting."

"It would be nice if the mystery was a simple bit of 'interesting,' " he admitted.

She chuckled. "Milord, the more interesting the mystery the more challenging it seems to be, and all the more rewarding at the end. There's always hope that this one person will have done it when all along we thought it was this other person over here. That's part of the fun!"

Derek nodded without comment, his thoughtful gaze not lifting as he stepped ahead of them down the hall. Mun and Para stared after him. She felt bad for him, mostly, because she needed to keep questioning him on his brother and Alicia Pomeroy. It gave her a foul taste in her mouth. She wished she could believe, with certainty, that Cyruss Kensington wasn't the guilty party. Well, a part of her did if for nothing but the priest's sanity. The more she heard about the elder Kensington and his warrior's ways, however, the more she grew certain he was somehow involved. *I'll need to give a question or three to Mun about things.* The warrior had a unique perspective on events.

Para's stomach grumbled. "Did we pass lunch?"

"Yes. It's coming close to three of the clock."

"Nefa's bright and shiny...." Para pressed her lips together before stalking forward. "Milord Priest, let us take a break and be done with the adventure for now. My center calls for a fill." She retrieved her leather cylinder of tools and opened the guest room door with ease. "This is as good a place as any to stop and take a meal, so, if you have no objections, let us make use of it."

Derek did an admirable job of shaking off his morose attitude, and he offered a smile as he followed her inside. Within was a large canopy bed, a balcony overlooking a pond and fountain, and a table with four chairs, all in a state of tumbled mayhem throughout the room.

Mun and Derek took to the task of retrieving the table and chairs while Para sought out unpleasant surprises. That done, she locked the door – she didn't like eating with doors wide open – and then set to the task of delving out bread and cheese. Mun had been in charge of the water and wine sacks, and these were now piled in the center of the table. All in all, it was a nice lunch, though late, for a day filled with adventuring – even if there wasn't enough action to suit Para.

"How long have you studied as a priest?" Mun inquired.

"Fifteen years."

Fifteen years seemed a very long time for someone to stare at musty old books while learning to pray in just the right way. And that only to get what they, or their patron lord, desired. Of course, it didn't seem much different than the Thief Guilds which catered to their own version of a 'patron lord'. As long as they had the coin, the Guild had the personnel to dole out, whatever the adventure.

"You made the decision very young to study the cloth," Mun said.

Derek nodded, offering the wine flask to Para. She accepted it. "I enjoyed books as a child, but I had no interest in studying spells and potions. The nearest Arcanist Guild was some distance away, and I had no intention of abandoning my family. So, I studied here at the church."

"Doesn't sound like much of a choice," Para grumbled.

"Understandably so, if one takes into account our seclusion. But I have enjoyed what they have sought to teach me, and they say I have a natural ability toward the healing arts. So, I do what I can where I am able."

"Without leaving the safety of home."

Mun sent Para a warning glare. She made a point of ignoring him.

"I don't stray far, no. But few priests do so. Sometimes there are those who find themselves venturing forth, usually in a large party of militia, but that is rare."

"Such being a blessing of residing under the Kensington banner?"

Nona King | 83

"To some a blessing; to others a curse," Derek observed.

"And which is it for you?"

The priest's expression grew thoughtful. "Being near family has never been viewed a curse, and recently I have begun venturing to the different hamlets under the Kensington banner. I don't view my studies as a curse, neither my family title. I suppose they could be viewed as limiting, to some, but they have also offered opportunity."

Para pulled apart a bit of cheese with thoughtful consideration. "Opportunity; it can be a bittersweet song sung in the ear."

"Indeed."

Opportunity flung windows wide while doors were left ajar, in Para's experience. A person had to be adept at understanding which was best to venture through. Most often an easy opportunity led to not-so-easy turns. Of course, there was often a gargantuan benefit at the resolve. Those, however, were few and far between. In fact, the last time she received such a reward had been in the cavern where she had met Mun. She nearly lost her life in that adventure, but it made her who she was today—a priceless commodity.

"Let us hope the prospect that rears its head here is taken for everything it has to offer… and then some," she said, meeting Mun and Derek's gaze each in turn. "One never knows the hand that's dealt, so let us choose to make it the most exciting hand of the night!"

Mun smirked. "Don't play cards with her," he warned the priest.

"No fair, giving up my secrets!"

Derek chuckled. "I thank you, Milord Meek, but I have quite the luck with cards. I would be amiss if I denied her the chance to fleece me, guilt free."

Para laughed. "That's the spirit, Milord! That's the spirit." She retrieved the deck of cards and the pair of dice from her pouches. "Which are you up for?"

The priest laughed again, Mun shaking his head in mild amusement. "Do we have time for a game, Mil—erm, Para? Surely we should continue on? We've only a few rooms left to wander."

"Why not call it a day early? The house isn't going anywhere, and the ghosts won't be out and about until this evening—if at all, with a priest about. Why don't we have a go, at least for an hour, and then continue on our way? Come along, be a sport!"

"Very well." He set aside his bit of cheese and bread and motioned to the dice. "Let me try my hand at those."

Mun heaved a sigh as Para explained the rules.

Derek caught on with rapid success for an alleged 'sheltered priest' who didn't venture often outside of the city limits. In fact, after six bouts of dice Para found herself on the low side of the points kept. It was then she began to wonder if he pulled a fast one to prove some type of point. After all, he could have spent most of his youth in soldiers' camps, thereby maturing into a gambling priest with a penitent for the healing arts.

Para regarded him through narrowed eyes as he took up the dice and shook them within the palm of his hand. "Come on seven!"

"Snake eyes," Mun corrected.

Derek's hand paused mid-action. "I want singles?"

Mun nodded.

"Ah. Come on snake eyes!" He chucked the dice into the center of the table, watching with intense concentration as they rolled to a stop on a single and a deuce. "Three."

"I've always been partial to four." The single shifted to another deuce of its own volition.

Para bolted from her chair, sending it crashing backwards as she let flow a stream of colorful language. Her eyes widened as they focused on the shimmering image of a ghost in a maid's

Nona King | 85

uniform standing just behind Derek. Mun, on the other hand, stood with deliberate slowness, taking time enough to shrug his shoulders and unlock his sword from its sheath. Derek peered over his shoulder and then spun, bolting to his feet and almost toppling the table.

"W-Who are you?" he stammered.

The ghost seemed shocked at their reaction and lowered her focus to her maid's uniform, as if to make certain she wasn't at all out of the ordinary. The only problem being she was *completely* out of the ordinary.

"I'm the maid Marina. I've come to clean the room for the mistress when she gets here."

"The mistress?" Para repeated. "Who?"

"Miss Pomeroy. She always comes, and it won't do to have her see her room like this." The maid tut tut'ed as she took to the task of retrieving those articles of paper and clothing scattered around the mussed bed.

Para watched with widened eyes. Focusing on Derek and Mun each in turn, she noticed their own thoughtful expressions. "You don't suppose…?"

"They say she haunts the mansion," Derek said as he sent a glance to the maid. "I never would have thought that the 'haunting' meant two ghosts."

"If this one prepares for her coming, perhaps she is soon due."

Para nodded as she hooked her thumbs on the belt of her scabbard. "If she comes and is as sentient as this one here, we could get some right good information from her about who did what." Marina the maid ghost began dusting while humming a haunting melody. "Who knew that ghosts would be so preoccupied with what used to be their earthly duties."

"Such devotion gives credence to Miss Pomeroy's reported character."

"I thought that myself." Para gave Derek's arm a jolt, drawing his attention. "Did you want to ask her some questions? Seems as if asking something of the dead is your thing and not ours."

"I've never… I can try." His focus was drawn again by the maid. Marina had paused her dusting to stare out the balcony toward the algae covered pond. "Miss Marina—"

"She comes."

Para, Mun, and Derek exchanged glances before scurrying to the balcony, hands gripping the baluster as they stared down at the pond below. All three made some type of holy gesture of protection at the vision they saw there: A young woman in flowing robes of white with tresses of loose dark hair. For several long moments she hovered above the pond near the fountain. Then she seemed to shift on a puff of breeze and began to step toward the brickwork path leading into the house.

The three watched her progress as long as they could before she was blocked by the balcony floor. Then they dove for the door and the hallway beyond, reaching the stairs and the railing in a fraction of the time one would have thought. However, no ghostly image of Miss Pomeroy was seen.

"We've got to find where she went," Para said, hurrying down the stairs.

Mun and Derek rushed after her, but all three came to an abrupt halt at the foot of the stairs when a voice filled with melancholy was heard to sing a haunting melody.

> *As the sun descends and the hues change to shadow*
> *My spirit stirs, but leaves me feeling Hollow*
> *For a time I fade, but then the night holds me completely*
>
> *This is not my home – I cannot stay*
> *Where is my home – Oh, so far away*
>
> *Alone in my room there comes upon me a shadow*
> *Trapped between these worlds I can't see who to follow*
> *Call to me so that I may cross over*
>
> *This is not my home – I cannot stay*

Where is my home – Oh, so far away

Eternal searching; Eternal fight,
Am I forgotten in this sea of night?
Endlessly prayerful through my watery mind
That I may recall whom I left behind

I chase after him, yet he cannot see me
As I pass through him, I know he has lost the feeling
I can feel him, but he cannot feel me

I have lost my home – forever astray
I have lost my home – can I return someday?

Lost and confused, the girl sought peace in her memories. That was all Para could reason based on what Marina had said. *Is she trapped in the last day of her life? ...perhaps.*

"Come on," she whispered, motioning ahead. "We didn't venture so far as the stables before. Perhaps she's gone that way? Mun, Derek, be ready. We don't know how much at peace she is at the moment."

Ghosts did odd things, and one never knew when they would choose to do them.

They made their way through the dining room and the study, hastening through the parlor and the game room to the outside patio. There, Para kept them back behind her as she unlocked the outer door and eased it open enough to observe the grounds just beyond.

"No ghost," she whispered.

Yet they could all hear the song as it continued to echo through the house, growing louder with each passing moment.

"Where in the—" She pressed her lips together and shifted her position for a better view of the outside. All she could see were the woods to the other side of the property and the brickwork path leading to the stables and corral. "Did she go somewhere else?" She felt a sudden grip on her arm and shifted her attention to the men behind her. Derek pointed through the rooms toward the ghostly presence approaching.

Para swore and scrambled with the others out the doors and down the brickwork path to the stables. They were clean, empty except for two saddles and tack made for light riding horses, and two bales of moldy hay with grass growing from the top and sides. They dove into the first empty stall and settled into silence, listening. *This is the oddest turn of events,* Para mused. But she would rather this experience than another run-in with a lich.

"Why don't we talk to her?" Derek hissed. "She sounds confused and lonely!"

"I'm not talking to her ghost until I know for certain she won't hand us our head, and you would do well to take that same position." She palmed a dagger as she peeked around the stall. The ghost of Alicia Pomeroy had just emerged from the outside patio. She ducked back behind the safety of the wall. "What is she doing? I thought she was here just a day before she went missing!"

"That's true, but she visited us here quite a few times before the betrothal announcement."

"Nefa's shiny..." Para grimaced. "So, what you're saying is there's no way to know where she's headed or why."

Derek sent her a sheepish glance, an answer in and of itself.

"While that tempts me to strike up a conversation, I think I'll leave well enough alone and eavesdrop instead." She tried not to admit that it was her hope to not need to eavesdrop on anything much more than the words of the song.

"I could try and speak to her," Derek insisted.

"Milord Priest..." Para fixed him with a meaningful scowl. "Derek, she might look like Alicia Pomeroy, but that out there is something a lot more dangerous, believe me. She's better left alone until we reason out what her mood is like, and even that could change at a moment's notice without warning. I understand you want to help your friend, and that's what we're here for, but rushing forth without an idea of what we're doing is the last thing to help."

Mun gripped the man's shoulder, drawing his distressed attention. "Milord, waiting is the better part of virtue at the moment. At least until we can determine what will be the most helpful to your friend. Patience."

Derek pressed his lips together, holding Mun's gaze for a long moment before shifting his focus away and releasing a long breath. He scrubbed at his scalp, wincing when his fingertips found the still tender portion of his scalp from the onslaught in the church.

"I'm sorry," he mumbled.

"You better set whatever aside right now, Milord Priest. We need your wits and your prayers."

He nodded, not lifting his gaze from their scrutiny of the ground at his feet. "They're yours, of course."

She hazarded a quick glance around the stall. "She's paused in the middle of the brickwork path on the way here." Para tugged at an ear lobe. "I hope she stops singing soon. It's giving me a severe case of the shivers."

Mun's somber expression didn't alter. "Where will we go should she venture this direction? The paddock?"

"As near as I can tell there should be a gate in the back of the stables here. We can dive out before she gets much closer, keeping an eye on her from the paddock. I'm hoping that when she doesn't see a mare she'll turn around and go back to the house."

One could always hope.

Para motioned to Derek and Mun while she once again peeked around the stall. "You two head through the gate first. I want to take a gander a little longer before I follow." She sent Mun a glance, intercepting his disapproving stare. "I'll be fine, Munwar. Now git."

After another moment of hesitation Mun nudged Derek out of the stall, utilizing the stable walls as cover from the ghost. Para watched them for an instant before focusing again on Alicia Pomeroy as she stood in the middle of the brickwork path halfway between the stables and the palace. The expression on the girl's face was blank, as if she had lost something and didn't understand where it had gone or how to get it back. The hair on Para's arms stood on end with the continued song, and her stomach curdled when the ghost's gaze fixed on the stable – exactly where she hid.

It didn't help matters that the song also came to a somewhat abrupt end.

With a hissed expletive, Para scrambled out the back of the stable, halting just around the side. Out of the corner of her eye she saw Mun and Derek at a small gate in the paddock fencing motioning her to continue toward them. Against her better judgment Para remained, casting a glance around the back of the stables to continuously gage the ghost's progress down the brickwork path. Once she had entered the stable, she began a light-hearted conversation—with no one.

Para's eyebrows arched upward and she hazarded a glance inside. Sure enough, Alicia Pomeroy stood in a stall talking to nothing. *Does she see a horse there?* Frowning, Para snuck back inside the stable, into the last stall, and as close as she could to the inner wall. She could just imagine the look of horror and irritation in Mun's stony gray gaze. But the change in position made the conversation a bit clearer, even though she could still only hear bits and pieces. With only one participant in what had previously been a two-sided conversation, the sense of it was lost.

Though it was a good sign when the young woman laughed, it wasn't such a good sign when Alicia Pomeroy ceased her conversation and began moving toward the back of the stables. With a glare to the heavens, Para's eyes darted from left to right for any avenue of escape, deciding on the small pile of hay to her left. She threw herself into the center and burrowed down, holding her breath and squeezing her eyes shut tight to prevent any other rustling once she settled.

Ghosts didn't have good hearing about earthly things, right?

The hay began to cause an itch at every part of her body, be it clothed or bare, after what seemed forever and a day. When she had decided that the next instant was her last, regardless of ghosts or goblins, she felt a firm grip around her ankle and squawked as she was forcibly yanked free from her hiding place.

She blinked up into Mun's annoyed expression and then offered a lopsided smile. "Tag, you're it?"

Derek, standing behind Mun, gave a shake of his head as he hid his amused smile.

The warrior straightened, his stern gaze enhanced by his fisted hands resting on his hips. "Did you want to solve the mystery of that young woman's haunting, or play childish games?"

She scoffed as she accepted Derek's help to stand. "Now, Mun, don't be like that. I only tried to hear a bit of conversation. I hoped to get a clue or three." Hay fell in clumps from her breeches, shirt, and hair as she looked about for the ghost. "Where did she get off to?"

Mun gestured toward the wood. "She ventured that direction."

"Into the woods?" Para asked, incredulous. "I don't care for the look of those particular woods."

Mun's focus shifted to them for a moment. "Why?"

"I don't know. They give me a sick feeling in the pit of my stomach."

This time it was Mun's turn to gape at her in incredulity. "You're a ranger."

"Of all the... Don't you think I realize how ridiculous it

sounds to be afraid of a bit of wood? But every time I look I get a case of the shivers and want to walk backwards. Of course we can go in there, we're supposed to solve this blasted mystery, but I'm just saying!"

Derek stepped between the two, fixing each with a calm stare of brown. "Milord Meek, Para, there is no need to enter the woods. If she is following a day in her life, she will return to the palace after her walk."

Para pointed at him, frowning. "Don't you give me an out, Milord Priest. By Nefa's bones I'll go in that wood and follow that wandering ghost!" To prove her point, she turned on her heel and stalked from the stable and down part of the brickwork path until she stepped off to head toward the wood.

Mun and Derek followed after her. She smacked herself on the back of the head, grumbling about giving too much credence to creepiness when there was a job to be done. She snatched the bow from across her back and an arrow from the quiver as she came to the border of the wood, pausing long enough to give Mun and Derek time to catch up to her.

"Don't be foolish," Mun said as he came to stand beside her.

"I'm a ranger. We go into woods." She sent him a glare. "I'm going in."

"And put us all in danger?"

"Bah! Don't use soft words to turn me over, Munwar Meek. We've been in tighter spots than this, and even if Milord Priest hasn't he's better with us in a creepy wood than in that house with whatever hides in the basement." Para faced the wood, adjusting her grip momentarily on the bow and the arrow before stepping deeper inside.

As was her usual custom her step was slow; her gaze diligent in its scrutiny of the flora, fauna, and earth as she sought to read the story it had to tell her. Her hatred of secrets went well with her skills as a ranger, as she took it upon herself as a personal challenge to be able to read and understand everything of her surroundings; regardless of whether her surroundings happened to be a city, a wood, a field, or a desert.

She kept clear of snow-peaked mountains—

Para knelt and tucked the arrow away, her now free hand reaching forward to caress the upturned earth. "No ghost passed by here, but something did. Something that wears a robe and soft-soled shoes." Eyes narrowing, Para scanned the surrounding area, her gaze falling on a patch of poppies that had recently been harvested, and a clump of aloe that had lost a few of its thick tendrils.

"Arcanist?" Mun asked as he crouched down beside her.

"It looks like, what with that room in the palace and now these." Para frowned and shifted her gaze behind them to the estate. "Milord Priest, what is your father doing with an experimenting arcanist added to the troop on yonder hill?"

"I don't know," he said, enhancing the statement with a full shrug.

"Could it be your brother? Although I don't know what an officer would do with anything from an arcanist. Well, I can't say that. If the arcanist is worth his salt, he can do a lot with weapons and armors to give a soldier a head start over everyone else. It's just that your brother, from what you've said, wouldn't be the kind to take anything like that. Hence the reason we found what we did." She heaved a sigh and straightened. "We need to corner the Lord Kensington, either your brother or father, and get some answers."

"I could send Father a letter via messenger," Derek offered.

"It may be quicker to seek the brother," Mun said. "He has an interest in the outcome of our search, be it his freedom or otherwise."

Para nodded, scrubbing at her scalp while missing her cap.

"Aye that. We should see to that tomorrow."

"Where has your brother journeyed?" Mun asked of the priest.

"Of that I'm not quite certain. He would often venture out to the surrounding cities to make certain affairs were still in order. I haven't seen or heard from him in more than a month."

"Explains the shambles of the palace," Para mumbled.

"Have there been reports of trouble from the other cities that would keep him?"

"He could have been kept by Father."

Para and Mun exchanged glances. "Where did your father get off to? One of the other cities around?"

Before Derek could answer the question Para felt the hairs on the nape of her neck stand at attention and shifted her gaze deeper into the wood, her focus fixing on the shimmering form of Alicia Pomeroy.

"It looks as though the walk is over," she observed. She gave Derek's arm a tug as she turned on her heel and headed out of the forest, the priest and warrior following on her heels. "Let's get ourselves to the outside patio until we can see for certain which way she's got it in her head to travel. We might need to split up a bit… though I can't say I'm all too thrilled with that notion."

She was concerned the priest would try to strike up a conversation with the girl.

"Par, I will wait at the crest of the stairs," Mun informed. "You and Derek can determine her route and give a signal if I need to change my location."

"I like it. Go ahead. Give a signal of your own if another surprise rears its head."

"Indeed." With that, Mun strode into the palace and disappeared from sight.

Para sent Derek an intense scrutiny. "Are you going to

behave yourself?"

Derek's countenance grew taut with a slight frown. "I will keep my distance."

"Hm." Para wasn't certain it meant the same thing, but she was willing to give him the benefit of the doubt for now. They entered the outside patio and Para directed him to the other side of the parlor and the 'resting room.' "Go make yourself scarce in there and keep an eye on which direction she takes. I'll stay here and keep an eye out until she gets into the palace."

He gave a nod and hurried to do so, settling himself behind the open door. Para herself ducked behind the open door of the outside patio, slinging the bow once again behind her back as she focused on the approaching visage of Alicia Pomeroy. *What story do you have to tell, miss? What did you see in your last minute that keeps you here?* Para frowned. *I hate secrets.* Unfortunately, sometimes it didn't matter how much she hated the untold story. The story remained untold, secrets stayed locked away, and she was cranky for at least a fortnight after. It was not a good time, for herself and Mun.

The last time she was unable to solve a mystery her crankiness had sent Mun to drink, and when he drank he grew philosophical and talkative. That had been an interesting experience for Para, a talkative warrior who was so sloshed that she couldn't understand but every fourth or fifth word. It was not something she wanted to repeat.

Alicia turned down the brickwork path toward the main entrance. Para frowned and hurried inside to give a whistle that drew Derek's peek around the door. She motioned toward the entry doors and then rushed through the patio to the game room. He acknowledged the change in direction and ducked back into hiding as she pressed herself against the wall to the right of the door leading into the parlor. It would be interesting to find out if Alicia stepped through the door or pushed it open.

The answer to the question was the groaning of the entry doors followed by a chill in the air and muffled steps on the hardwood floors. Para knew the noise would alert Mun to the girl's approach and allow him to plan appropriate stealth. She didn't know yet what they intended to do other than follow the ghost to see what she revealed. Any information at this point would be helpful to give them another place to start on the morrow, even if that was talking with Lord Pomeroy, tracking down Cyruss, or sending a message to Lord Kensington.

Para risked a slight peek around the door frame— and swore when she saw the girl turn into the resting room. Before she could decide on an action, the ghost passed beyond the door of Derek's hiding place and halted, turning her face toward the exact location of the priest.

Eight

The change to the girl's countenance drained the blood from Para's face and sent her rushing forward as she drew her sword and yelled for Mun at the top of her lungs. The girl screeched and dove at the priest, such a look of rage and vengeance giving Para a fright even as she intercepted the attack and deflected it as best she could while yelling at Derek to "Run!" when he continued to stand there in stupefied amazement.

Mun charged down the stairs and around the corner, drawing the girl's attention long enough for Para to shove Derek hard in the side with her shoulder to get him moving. "Run, damn it!" she yelled, punctuated by a slap to the face to grab his attention.

This time his eyes flickered with awareness and he turned on his heel and ran.

Alicia didn't notice his going, so focused on Mun and the harm threatened by his large claymore. Once Derek had escaped Para shouted, "Move back!" and the pair began to manipulate the angry yet frantic ghost out of the resting room. When they stood fully in the parlor, Alicia fled up the stairs, her weeping causing chills.

"What in Nefa's ass," she grumbled between great puffs of breath. She sheathed her sword, Mun doing the same as they focused on the staircase at the far end of the house—a shrill, terrified scream shook the walls of the house and propelled the two up the stairs at a dead sprint. They didn't stop until they crashed through the partially opened door of the guest room and charged for the balcony.

Looking down, Para swore. The water of the fountain situated in the center of the pond had reddened, and that color began to dwindle. It had almost vanished when she made out the form of Derek coming to stand at the water's edge, his shoulders hunched and his head lowered as if in prayer. He slumped to his knees.

She pushed from the baluster, eyes wide as she vigorously rubbed her scalp. "Munwar," she said in a very low voice, "I do believe we might have bitten off a bit more than we intended."

Mun, who continued to stare down at the pond below, inclined his head. A frown furrowed his brow.

"What are you thinking?" she prompted.

"Did you note her reaction?"

Para scoffed. "I was in the middle of it, Mun."

This time he turned and met her gaze. "That isn't what I meant. Her countenance. Her action. Did you note that response to Milord Priest?"

"Aye." Para sent a troubled glance toward the balcony. "Toward the end of the fracas she looked to be a trapped cat. But that first lunge… it had all the reading of a woman on the attack."

"For vengeance."

"Aye." Para lifted her finger. "Before you go along on that track, Munwar, just keep it aside."

"It is a possibility," he pressed.

"Just so, but it's one of many."

"Day one is premature for accusations," Mun agreed, "but we need to acknowledge every suspect."

"And he is a good'un, isn't he? Friends with the girl, irritated at his brother's handling of her… the fact that he's lingered around here is a tick to his innocence, but even so…."

"His remaining could be out of guilt and a need for atonement?"

Para frowned as she let out a fast breath. "I'm all for escaping this place tonight and sleeping at the inn in a soft, warm bed without the worry after ghosts and ghouls, or visitors from the basement. What say you?"

Mun nodded, stepping once more onto the balcony to peer below. "We should gather Milord Priest. He seems distraught."

"Aye." Para stood beside the warrior to take note of Derek's current frame of mind. He still knelt at the water's edge, but this time his hands were folded in prayer and a soft aura of white seemed to radiate from him. "You don't suppose our lord priest has been experimenting with ways to bring her back, do you?"

Mun shook his head. "I do not, but I don't have any reason why."

"Just doesn't seem his character?" Para shrugged and turned from the balcony. She gathered their flasks and lunch from the table. "This is a puzzle indeed, Mun. It's my hope we can look back on this bit of adventure and have a good laugh."

The warrior continued to stare below. "This adventure will lead a good many places," he observed solemnly.

Her eyebrow twitched upward at the philosophical statement from him while sober. She had noted more of those of late. "The bed beckons my name, Milord Meek." She gestured for the open door into the hall. "After you."

With one last look below, he passed her to the hallway beyond. The pair made their way through the first floor rooms toward the pond on the side of the palace. Para caught herself searching her surroundings for any sight of Miss Pomeroy, though there was no reason why she should believe the girl would return. Regardless, Para kept her hand on the pommel of her sword and noticed Mun doing much the same.

The duo circled around the front of the house to the pond just as Derek stood. His focus remained on the fountain. Mun and Para kept their distance for a long moment, giving him what time he may have needed to sort through the thoughts that weighed upon his shoulders. It was the first time Para remembered seeing him distressed. Yes, she had only met him a short time ago, but the impression she had gathered of him was that of a cheerful sort.

She sent Mun a sidelong glance before stepping forward to rest a hand on the priest's shoulder. His muscles twitched, but he didn't look away. "We're off to town, Milord Priest. You're welcome to join us."

He took in a slow breath before forcing a smile and shifting his gaze to meet hers. "Thank you. I believe I shall. The inn?"

Para nodded, lowering her hand as they began the trek back to town. There were so many questions rising to the forefront that she had a bit of a challenge to keep them at bay and let the silence be. The silence continued even when the trio entered the inn, gathering in the furthest corner of the common room and doing their best to stay out of earshot from those few who lingered that late.

Para ordered three mugs of hot cider and then resumed her scrutiny of her nails while doing her best to keep silent. If she opened her mouth, questions would spew forth and now wasn't necessarily the best time. After a shock such as what they had just been through? No. Their wits should be left as much alone as they could at the moment, leaving everything for the morning and a clear head.

She wasn't too eager to get back into the palace at the moment either.

The best bit would be to get some questions answered by Milord Pomeroy. Maybe he's heard a tale or two about where the brother has got himself off to? If not, then they would seek out the Lord Kensington and see what he had to say about anything. Lords of noble houses generally liked keeping tabs on all that went on in their family, good or otherwise. The only thing being he wouldn't necessarily want to volunteer that information to a pair of travelers, even if they were able to get Derek to go along with them.

Para accepted her hot cider and focused on the amber liquid as she breathed in the tangy apple aroma. The warmth of the mug was like embracing a comforting fire, and it made her realize how sleepy she was. In fact, after a few sips her eyelids began to grow heavy and she had to fight the temptation to take a nap there upon her forearm… and the room faded to black.

༺§༻

"She's waking."

It was Mun's voice that spoke through the fog, but she couldn't lift her head or hands to push away the gods-awful smell that lingered at her nose. Choking and sputtering, she struggled to open her eyes to focus on the brown ones that didn't look at all familiar…. *Wait.* "Derek?"

The priest smiled, his eyes registering relief. "Welcome back."

"What in Nefa's blood is going on? Why do I feel like I'm on the south end of an elephant?" She struggled to push herself into a seated position, immediately noticing that she lay on the floor of the common room. "What in the— what is going on?"

"The cider was poisoned."

Para's gaze snapped to Mun, her eyes narrowing. "Say again?" She accepted Derek's help to sit up.

"Someone poisoned your drink," Derek said. "I haven't tested the others yet."

Mun motioned to the priest. "If not for Priest Derek, you would have been as Miss Pomeroy."

A flame of temper sparked. "Please tell me you beat the barmaid half way to death and back again."

Mun smirked. "We have no proof she is responsible."

"I don't give a whit who's responsible!" She stumbled to her feet, the room doing an odd shift that sent her staggering backwards. Derek steadied her. "If someone is trying to poison us, then my hands around their throat will be reason enough for them to want us dead: Fear for their own life."

"You should rest," Derek told her as he tried to get her to sit. "You aren't making sense."

"Bah!" Para attempted to push his hands away but only succeeded in sending herself off balance and nearly falling backwards.

"Par, sit," Mun ordered.

She glowered at him but complied.

"I will question the barmaid and any other in the kitchen. You will be led upstairs by Milord Priest and go to bed so you can recover."

"I—"

"Par."

Her mouth clicked shut as she continued to glare at his stern countenance, his stony gaze not easing one bit.

"Para," Derek said, "the medicine can only continue to work you free from the poison if you rest."

Grumbling, she acquiesced and allowed herself to be led upstairs into her room. It took her quite a time to make it up the stairs, growing winded and dizzy after only three or four steps and needing a rest. Derek urged her to take her time, and at one point near the top she could have sworn that he wore the luminescent glow she had seen at the pond while he prayed for Alicia Pomeroy. The direct result was a lessening to the dizziness and the nausea and being able to reach her bed.

Derek helped her off with her boots and then arranged the

covers over her. "Rest now. I will check on you later to ensure the poison is gone."

"Turn about is fair, eh?" she asked as he turned away.

He faced her again, smiling. "It seems so, doesn't it?"

"Don't think you will keep me abed in the morning, Milord Priest."

"Of course not. Now rest. Milord Meek and I will question the staff."

"You do that, and don't let him be soft on them," she called after his exiting figure.

He shut the door without comment.

Para frowned at the door and then the ceiling. Lacing her hands behind her head, she wondered what the three of them could have found, or done, to cause a vial of poison to be upset into their ciders. An attempt at taking a life was a serious matter, and the fact of that wasn't lost on her. It only made her grip tighter onto the determination to solve the mystery that whispered from every corner of the palace on yonder hill.

Nine

Para cradled her head in her hands, her eyes closed against the sunlight and the noise of the common room as Priest Derek went to fetch something that would supposedly help the piercing ache. She could feel Mun's regard of her pale complexion and knew that he entertained the thought of leaving her behind as they went to the town of Arielle to question Cyruss Kensington.

Truth be told, she was in no mood or capacity to travel by horse for any amount of time. Rising from bed that morning had caused an avalanche of pain from the top of her scalp to the tips of her toes, eliciting a groan of agony and a desire to vomit. It had taken much goading with her inner child to get her to stand and almost stumble down the stairs. When Priest Derek and Munwar saw her condition, the priest had immediately ventured out into the city for something to help. Mun had wrangled them a table as far from the aromas of the kitchen as he could manage without moving the table onto the front porch.

Now she sat nearest the window and began to wish for death, if for nothing else but to free herself from the unseen knife that pressed against her right eye and into her brain. Even the thought of speech made her stomach gurgle and forced a belch from her lips that smelled as rank of death.

Para moaned and rubbed at her forehead.

"You should try to drink something."

"…no," she said after a momentary revulsion.

"I can have them make something that will—"

She slammed the flat of her hand against the table without lowering her other from the duty of shielding her eyes from the morning light.

Mun heaved a sigh. "You should stay here as Priest Derek and I venture to Arielle."

It was the truth; the truth of all truths at that point. If Derek and Mun happened upon anything of trouble, to say nothing of a fracas with the brother, she would only make matters worse and get one of them killed—the way her adventure was going, it would be her body that would drop.

Her finger began to tap a morose rhythm on the table-top.

"I understand you don't wish to be outside the investigation," he said. "You could use this time to discover more information from Lord Pomeroy."

Killing two avenues with one journey, Para knew it was the best solution to the current problem. It also afforded her the chance to sleep off the remaining effects of the poison and keep herself from attempting to pick a fight with someone who would guarantee she would be put out of her misery. At the way her head pounded, she would gouge her own brain out with a spoon just to get it to stop.

Para risked a slight incline of head, but even that caused explosions behind her eyes. Groaning, she brought her other hand back up to help with the holding of her aching head. She didn't even drink enough ale to get this type of misery the morning after. When she discovered the culprit who had tipped the vial, she would do the same to them and enjoy the watching as they re-lived her agony.

Death would be merciful compared to what she wanted to do to them.

Priest Derek entered, then, carrying a pair of tapered candles. If she was going to be expected to journey back up the stairs to her room and burn those while she slept, there was no way Nefa himself would get her to cooperate. She would rather jump into a burning vat of oil than stand at the moment.

"These should help," Derek said as he sat beside her.

The slight jolt sent a wave of agony through her head and invited a moan.

"Ah. Forgive me, Para." He set the extra candle down and set to searching his pockets. Mun pulled a flint and steel from his pouch and offered it forward. "Thank you, Milord Meek."

The priest lit the first candle with ease, gauging its flame to prevent sputtering. He then dripped the first few drops of hot wax onto the table and pressed the base of the candle into it to keep it steady. The aroma of the candle was a spicy sweetness that initially caused Para to dry heave. But after the first shock, her stomach settled down and ceased its grumbling.

"If your head aches even after the second candle burns, have the inn keeper fetch Lord Pomeroy's herbalist immediately." Derek sent a glance toward Mun. "Will you be well enough to light the second candle, Para?"

She only risked a slight lift of her finger.

"All right." He pulled something from his pocket wrapped in a piece of cloth and set it on the table just in front of her. "Try and eat all of these before this evening, as it will help fight off the poison."

He pulled back a flap to reveal a collection of small coin-shaped morsels of food. If her head hadn't felt as if it would fall off her shoulders at any moment, she would have been able to identify if it was tuber, grain, or something similar. So, Para only lifted the same finger as before in understanding.

"Come along, Milord Priest. We had best go now. It is a long journey to Arielle."

"Coming." Derek rested a hand on her shoulder with a careful lightness of one familiar with treating the ill. "The first one you eat, suck it as long as you can taste the flavor. Then chew very slowly, letting the juice build up in your mouth until you can't hold more. Try and swallow the juice only a portion at a time then. If you can do that with more than one, that would be best. All right?"

They may have been the oddest instructions she had ever heard in her life, but it wasn't entirely different from some herbal treatments she had learned in her travels. It could amaze a person what a bit of leaf could do for what ails.

The inn door clicked shut behind the pair, leaving Para alone to her misery—which was preferred. The first candle did set aside her desire to vomit at the smell or thought of food which, she felt, was a marked improvement. It was after she lit the second candle that she braved the eating of her first coin-sized bit of mystery, following the instructions set down by Priest Derek as best she could remember. Her stomach felt well enough that she risked a second and then a third, deciding to pause after that for fear of putting herself back into a miserable state.

The second candle caused the pain in her head to dwindle enough, also, that she was able to risk an alteration to a more comfortable position—that being resting her head on her forearms. Quite a few times a curious inhabitant of the common room approached her table to ask if she needed help. But they were quickly ushered away by the inn keeper, who must have been left explicit instructions by Mun to keep her alone and unbothered.

It was a nice thought to be so well cared for, even if they had left her behind.

When Para gauged the pain in her head manageable enough, she peeked outside the window to get the time. It was just past noon. Yawning, Para pressed her hands onto the table top and pushed herself to her feet, preparing herself for the possible onslaught to her head. The reaction was minimal at worst, which caused her a smile and sigh of relief.

If anyone hated being out of commission more than she did, she hadn't met them yet.

She wrapped the remaining bits of mystery food in their cloth and tucked them in her belt pouch, fingering one for a moment's consideration before popping it in her mouth. Then she took up the remaining portion of candle and slipped it into her pouch as well. She wanted to have everything near at hand that had brought her back to the land of the painless.

Trekking her way to Lord Pomeroy's mansion, she continued to send glances over her shoulder toward the noon sun as it fell on Kensington Palace. How they would arrange to talk to Miss Pomeroy she had no idea, unless it meant leaving Derek back at the church. *And how do you get someone like him to sit and twiddle his thumbs?* That would be the question of the hour, when it finally came to the doing of the deed.

The same maid as before greeted her at the entry of the Pomeroy mansion and ushered her into the same parlor. Para accepted the offer of chilled water and drank the first half of the glass before even pausing for a breath. The maid refilled the glass and then left to summon her master. Para took the opportunity to scrutinize the room. For what, she wasn't certain, but she took the moment regardless. And it was in that scrutiny she noted a recently opened letter on the writing desk in the corner.

"Lord Pomeroy will be with you in a few minutes," the maid informed.

Para nodded, fingering her glass as she listened to the muffled step of the maid as she ascended the stairs. Then she stood and stepped nimbly to the writing desk, adjusting her view so that she could read the letter without adjusting its position. Her eyes widened and she very nearly snatched the papers up in her shock.

Hearing the robust sound of a heavy door closing, Para returned to her seat and her glass of water, wiping the ring from the table while sending a grimace in the direction of the parlor door. Lord Pomeroy arrived a few moments later.

"Ah. Ranger Sedi. What can I do for you?" he asked as he sat in the chair across from her.

The title 'Ranger Sedi' caused a twitch to her right eyebrow. "I've a question or three of the younger Lord Kensington."

"Derek?"

"Hm? Oh. No. Not the younger." Para's cheeks flushed as she frowned with irritation at her own blunder. "Sorry. Out of sorts this morning. I meant Cyruss."

"Ah." Lord Pomeroy lowered his gaze to the tips of his fine leather shoes, his hands gripping each arm of the chair. "An interesting lad, Cyruss Kensington. Gifted in military matters, though I believe it was more his determination that caused him to succeed. Cyruss Kensington did not accept failure of any kind from himself or from those around him."

"An interesting individual to pair with a daughter such as I've heard tell of Alicia," Para observed, her eyes narrowing to gauge his reaction.

His hands tightened a bit on the arms of the chair. "Indeed, I suppose that could be said in truth. His attitude seemed to loom over her innocence much like a dark and angry cloud, though that never daunted her brightness. She had resilience of a separate kind, Alicia did."

"So, you arranged this marriage with Lord Kensington and got it all put to rights through Lord Cyruss?"

"Put to rights?"

"He agreed?"

"The arrangement was made."

"An arrangement can be made with one and not agreed to by

the other. Causes a bit of friction." Para crossed her arms as she regarded Lord Pomeroy's darting gaze. "I've heard from Priest Derek that his brother had told you all he wanted nothing of the match. Did you get that bit of information before sending Alicia on her way?"

"Cyruss..." Lord Pomeroy pressed his lips into a thin line as his gaze hardened. "Lord Kensington and I made an arrangement."

"We've got that, Milord. What I'm getting at is if the elder had the same arrangement in mind that you thought you had with him. Let's say... perhaps he had a different skirt in mind for the vows? A different face for the veil?"

Lord Pomeroy's brows furrowed until they met. "Ranger Sedi, there was—"

"An arrangement. Right," she interrupted as she stood. "So, you've made a pact to cease a war and may have blown the war into a new level of horror with your meddling." She touched her forehead with a finger in salute. "Milord, thank you for the tale."

She left the mansion in a sour mood, but at least her head didn't linger on the boundary of exploding inside her skull and her stomach seemed happier than it had been in months. Popping another bit of the mystery food, she passed the inn and continued toward the Kensington palace, telling herself she only wanted to tour the grounds and wouldn't go beyond the entry doors... much—

There was a minimal pull at her belt pouch, which caused a quick swipe of her hand to the offender and pulled up a small arm attached to a 'little shrub.' "Henry?" Her eyes widened as she set the sylvan back on his feet and accepted her bit of candle back from him.

He grinned innocently up at her. "Hi."

"Henry Sidgwick, what are you doing here?"

"Looking here and there for things to do. No one wants to

go anywhere any more these days." His frown made him appear even more like a child.

She sent the palace a look. "Doing things like what?" He had been handy on their journey to Pomeroy, so who was to say he wouldn't continue to be handy inside of a haunted mansion? Maybe he had more of those smoke bomb type tricks?

"Whatever they need me to do," he said accompanied by a shrug. Then his eyes brightened. "Do you need anything?"

"Maybe, but I don't know what you can do."

"Take me with you and I'll show you!"

"Hm." She crossed her arms as she regarded his over-eager expression. The sylvan stood on his tiptoes with his eagerness to be a part of whatever adventure she had going on. It was pathetic and endearing at the same time. "How good are you at finding secrets?"

His face screwed up in confusion. "Secrets? Like what humans say to one that they don't want said to another?"

"Well… well, there's that too, but I'm meaning hidden doors, traps… things like that."

"Oh! That! Psh!" He waved a hand. "Child's play. I could do that with my eyes closed."

"Hm. That so?" The sylvan nodded. Para shrugged. "I suppose there's nothing but to go ahead." She gestured toward the palace in the distance. "We're heading up there to have words with a ghost. You up for that?"

Henry's eyes grew wide like saucers. "A ghost? Truly?"

"As sure as I'm standing here."

"So it's true?"

Para's right eyebrow arched. "What is true?" She wrapped an arm around his shoulder and drew him forward. "You've heard something about this haunting, Henry?"

"Just that she sings a lovely song. I want to hear her song." He pulled his flute from his pouch. "I could play along and make her feel better."

"Maybe figuring out the song will make her feel better?" If she sang the song every night and it was the same.... Para shrugged it off. *A clue couldn't be that easy, could it?* There wasn't even any certainty that Miss Pomeroy wouldn't attack again. It was simply a guess based on bits of information… the best way to go, really.

"We're going to be there all night with her?"

"I don't know about that. You know how Munwar is, and he doesn't want me here by myself."

"But that's why I'm here!"

Para patted his back. "Just so, Master Henry. Just so. With you here everything is right as it should be. Now, do you need to stop by anywhere and be refreshed before we head on up the rest of the way?"

He lifted a flask slung across his small form. "I have my refreshment right here."

"Good lad. So let us be on our way and see what there is to see, shall we?"

The two made their way beyond the main street of the city and headed toward the main palace gates. The sun was still in the light of the early afternoon, so Para had a bit of time to investigate the grounds before the possibility of Alicia's arrival. The most important point Para wanted to see was the pond and the crumbling fountain in the middle.

All day she remembered the fading sight of the reddened water, wondering if there was something in the foliage that would cause the reddening at just the right place and time. Never mind the fact that it had been eerily similar to the red of freshly spilled blood. How did a ghost bleed? It was impossible, which meant there had to be another explanation. She only needed to figure out what it could be.

Easy enough, right?

Para led Henry to the pond as she confessed the adventure of the previous day. No sense in eliciting the elf's help and then keeping him in the dark about what went on. The more help the better, and especially if the help was… well, helpful.

"This is where she appeared yesterday," Para said, pointing to the fountain. "Just there, all flowy and ghost-like while singing her song."

"Did you hear any of it?"

"A bit, but I didn't pay attention enough to remember it today."

Henry grimaced and focused again on the fountain. Then he scrambled down the bank of the pond, sitting there on the edge as his legs dangled into the water. "How deep is it, I wonder? I want to look at the fountain."

"You and me both." Para regarded the depth of the pond. "I think I could trek across with no issue, if you want to sit on my shoulders."

Henry agreed, much to her surprise, and heaved himself up onto her shoulders with relevant ease. The sylvan, while he didn't weigh much, still made the duty of going down into the pond an interesting affair considering the slickness of the grass after a light drizzle during the day. Para had to pay attention how she stepped even more so than she had intended. It wouldn't do for Mun and Derek to return to find her laid up with a broken leg or arm, or both. She wouldn't hear the end of it from either of them for the remainder of the month at least.

"Can you get down onto the fountain?" Para asked him, reaching up a hand.

"Of course!" He grabbed hold of her hand and somehow swung free of her shoulders to land with ease on the marble fountain. He grinned at her. "See?"

Para smirked. "You're a crazy little shrub."

"Don't call me a shrub!" he protested.

"All right, all right, Milord Sylvan. I apologize. Now, you look around that side and I'll meet you 'round the other."

"What am I looking for?"

"Anything that is out of the ordinary I suppose would be the best way to say it."

He wrinkled his nose. "That seems silly, but I'll look."

"Obliged." Para removed her leather gloves and began her dutiful examination of the portions of the fountain. At times she would close her eyes and focus even more on what her fingers sought. Unfortunately, neither she nor Henry found anything of any significance. Needless to say, she was disappointed.

"Are we going inside?"

Para regarded the sky to determine the time. "Three o'clock. I suppose we could pop in for a quick search. Not down to the dungeon yet, though. We need to save that bit of excitement for Milord Meek."

"Is there something down there?"

Para led the sylvan to the front entry doors. "Milord Priest heard a sound from the kitchens."

"Who's that?"

"The priest? Oh, aye, you haven't met him yet, have you? Derek Kensington."

Henry's eyes widened. "Him?"

Para's eyebrows twitched upward. "What do you mean 'Him?' and said like that? Can't quite tell if you're disturbed or just know the man."

"Nothing, it's just..." Henry looked away. "Nothing."

"Henry, I don't think you quite get what we're trying to accomplish here. You're not supposed to hold onto secrets from me. We're to find the secrets together."

The sylvan laughed. "I know that," he protested.

"Then why don't you tell me what has you surprised about our lord priest?"

"It's just… a lot of the people here whisper how they believe he's the one that… that killed her."

"And just why is that?" She had been trying not to toy with the same idea since yesterday.

"They say he was in love with her and didn't want her to marry his brother."

"Bah!" Para grimaced. "A priest isn't one to murder, and not for love's sake either, Milord Sidgwick. They're sworn to celibacy, if you remember. And, if anything, he would pop his brother and not the girl. Gents have a thing with protecting the innocent, aye?" These were the same reasons she had been repeating to herself on multiple occasions.

"I'm just telling what they say." He shrugged. "You humans do funny things."

"Aye that, Milord, aye that. Like a bit of a mystery on the second floor: An experiment room for an arcanist. Have you ever seen one of those before?"

"An arcanist?" Henry scoffed. "Of course I have."

"No, no. Not an arcanist. An experiment room."

"Yes, but they usually don't smell good," he complained, pinching at his nose.

Para laughed, remembering a peculiar odor that had hung in the air. "Aye, they don't smell much like flowers, do they? Makes you wonder why an arcanist would stay so long in the little rooms, doesn't it?"

Henry nodded.

Para pushed open the front entry and then peeked around the doors. In search of what she wasn't sure, but it made her feel better to make certain there wasn't *some*thing waiting for innocent souls to step inside.

"Are we going to look all around again? You've seen it already, right?" Henry asked, looking around the parlor with wide eyes.

"Aye. I've seen it most all, but we can take a turn around

if you're curious. Did you want to do that?" The sylvan could possibly find something she had missed, after all.

"Could I see where you saw the ghost?"

Nodding, she ushered him through the parlor and the dining hall to the stairs leading to the second story. The experiment room is up here as well, if you're wanting to see."

"Oh no. No thank you. At least, not yet," he amended.

Para chuckled. "All right, Milord Sylvan. It's up to you, like I said. Everything is open 'round here, so it's easy enough to open a door and take a peek inside. Speaking of which…." She opened the door to the guest room beyond the private library where they had met Marina and then Alicia Pomeroy. "This would be the room."

Henry poked his head around the door to gauge the condition of the room; the turned down bed, the messy floor, and the open glass doors leading onto the balcony to a view of the pond and fountain. Satisfied that it was empty of threats, he came around the door and headed for the bookshelf on the far corner of the room.

"Looking for something, Master Henry?"

"I never know until I find it," he confessed.

Something that Para could completely understand. She didn't understand why life could be like that, either, because it certainly made things a definite challenge when they didn't necessarily need to be that way.

"We could ask Marina, if she shows up again."

"Who's that?" Henry asked, still searching the books on the shelves.

"She's the other ghost we met."

Henry spun, eyes wide. "There are two ghosts?"

"Oh yes. This is quite the lively place in the late afternoon and evening: ghosts, ghouls, arcanists experimenting on who knows what… It's a denizen of villainous activity."

Nona King | 119

Henry regarded for a long moment before laughing and saying his usual, "You're funny," while pointing at her.

Para sighed. "Aye. There is that." At least she didn't have an audience for the accusation. She sat at the table and pulled out her dice, remembering how the game the night before had drawn Marina out. "Would you like to play a game, Master Henry?"

He cast a sidelong glance. "I don't like playing with you."

"Come on now! I promise to give you a head start this time. Just one or two rolls. We won't even take down points. Just for practice."

"Oh all right." He ambled from the shelves to the table and pushed himself up. "What are we playing?"

"Are dice all right with you, Master Henry? We've tried your hand at cards already, so…."

"I don't know any dice games."

"That isn't a problem. I'll teach you my favorite."

"But how do I know you're teaching me right!"

Para stared at him, slack-jawed. "Master Henry! I would never lead you astray. Not with games of chance!"

Henry regarded her through narrowed eyes. "You like winning."

She laughed. "Everyone likes winning, Master Henry. Even you! That's why you're so grumpy."

He shrugged. "Oh all right. What are the rules?"

"Simple enough, Milord Henry. Simple enough." As Para explained the pattern of sevens or singles, the hair on the back of her neck lifted and a tingle shot down her spine. There was no song, so she doubted it was a case of Miss Alicia Pomeroy returning to her nightly haunt. Instead, she began to wonder if it was a case of the ghosts watching while trying to reason why this same silly ranger was again in their house.

She had found herself wondering the same thing upon occasion.

But when she thought of the young Miss Pomeroy and the too soon demise suffered at the hand of someone… there was no turning away from the solving of this mystery. As Derek Kensington had said, Miss Alicia deserved peace and the only way to give her that was to solve the riddle of her disappearance.

And if that's the very same Derek Kensington?

That question would need to be dealt with once they came to that particular answer. At the moment, she hesitated to place complete blame on him, although she wouldn't be able to offer a reason why—like Munwar. The priest's guilt could be the reason someone had been sent to kill him when they first met in the church. Of course, his seeking the guilty party could have caused the same attack.

And what of the fact that the elder Kensington didn't want to marry the girl? That he is now wed to someone else in a neighboring city? Or so read the letter upon Lord Pomeroy's desk, and from the officer himself. It rubbed Para raw, the fact that the girl was wronged and done away with and now the Kensington's hid the secret within their own noble family. It gave her a bad taste in her mouth for those of royal lineage. *Now, Par,* she scolded, *sure enough it seems the Kensingtons did the deed, but you don't know that for certain and can't put that for a fact until you do know. It could be the experimenting arcanist!* An arcanist who currently resided in the Kensington palace. She scrubbed at her scalp with such ferocity that she hissed an expletive.

"Isn't that what I was supposed to get?" Henry asked, his eyes wide as he stared across the table at her.

"Hm? Oh, sorry, Milord Sylvan. I was trapped in a thought."

"The mystery is bothering you?"

"Just so, Milord. Just so."

"I like puzzles," Henry offered. "A good one will keep me happy for days before I solve it, and then I get bored again."

"Have you tried your hand at this Kensington-Pomeroy bit

of puzzlement?"

He shrugged but sent her a telling glance.

"It has you stymied, doesn't it, Milord?"

"No, it doesn't," he huffed. "I don't care to know who did what is all."

Chuckling, she gestured with one hand. "Come along, Henry. Tell the tale of what you've discovered. Have you found anything out from Lord Cyruss?"

"Don't talk about him," he said, frowning.

"Oh really now? What has you in a tizzy about Lord Cyruss?"

"He's an angry man, that's what. Doesn't talk to anyone nicely about anything. I only asked one question and he jumped at me like I bit his leg. Took me up by my scruff and threw me outside!"

Both Para's eyebrows shot upward in shocked wonder. "And what question put him in such a temper?"

"I only asked him if he believed what they were saying about his brother!" In a huff now, Henry crossed his arms as his brows furrowed still. "He is a very angry man, and I don't like him very much at all."

"Now that's an interesting reaction indeed," Para mused. "What do you think, Milord? Was it out of guilt, or because he believes the rumor?"

"I'm sure I don't care," he told her. He snatched up the dice and gave them back to her. "I don't want to play anymore."

"Oh come along, Milord Henry," she said as she accepted the dice. "Don't be such a child about the thing."

"Such a tantrum for such a handsome boy." The feminine voice sounded behind them, and both focused on the ghostly visage of the maid Marina.

Ten

Para's reaction was much the same as before, but without the excessive expletive use. Henry, also, had quite the frightful reaction, leaping from his chair to the table and nearly falling backwards off of that. Pointing at the ghost, Henry spluttered for a full minute before going silent.

"Miss Marina," Para complained in a harsh tone, "could you stop with the appearing out of nothing to give us a fright!" Then her mind grabbed at the fact that the last time Marina appeared, it wasn't but a few minutes later that Miss Pomeroy had made her entrance. "Nefa's bones…. What time is it? It's not time for the miss to show, is it?"

"Oh no," Marina assured. "She's not due for a time. I still need to have the cook prepare her dinner, and look at this mess!"

Henry continued to stare, wide-eyed. *He's not seen a ghost before?* She thought for certain he would have seen a ghost once or twice in the span of his life, even if he was young… for an elf. Para helped him off the table, chuckling to herself when his gaze didn't waver from the female ghost maid as she went to the task of straightening the room.

"Marina, do you mind if I ask you a few questions? I'll even help you put the room to rights."

Marina straightened, her pretty face showing mild confusion.

"Questions about what, pray? I'm but a maid. Wouldn't you rather question the miss when she comes? She knows so much more than me about anything."

"You like the miss, do you?"

"Oh yes," Marina agreed with a bright tone, "she's wonderful. It's no wonder the master has taken to her so."

"The master? Lord Kensington senior?"

"Oh no. Milord Derek. He's such a gentle man, and the two are like birds of a feather."

"Birds of a feather, eh?" Para rested her hands on her hips, a finger absently tapping against her breeches. "What did the elder Kensington brother think of them getting along so wonderful? A bit jealous at all was he? Did he take to her about as well as his brother?"

If it were possible, the ghostly visage of maid Marina paled and then flushed. She turned away to busy herself with the straightening of the room. "We don't speak of him here," she said crisply.

The aura of the room seemed to chill, causing a shiver from Para and jolting Henry from his shocked stupor. "He isn't well thought of all the way 'round, is he?" she asked.

"He's an officer," Marina offered by way of explanation, and her tone was downright haughty.

"An officer that made the feuds stop in the other cities," Para reminded.

Marina stomped her foot, her hands fisted at her sides. "He's a violent man, he is, and tantrums if he isn't given what he wants, much like a child instead of a grown man. No peace will come to him until he comes to it, and this is what I believe!" With that, the ghost maid stormed from the room and was heard to cry as she fled down the hall.

Para took off after her, turning long enough to hiss a command to Henry and get him to scurry after her. As ghosts are wont to do, Marina held no respect for doors to be opened and closed, so Para wasn't completely certain where she had got off to.

"For the bones of…" Para pressed her lips together as she gripped the banister of the stairs with a hand, the other scratching at the back of her neck. "On the off-chance that she's lingering here abouts, I suppose we open each door we see. What say you, Milord Sidgwick?"

"She scares me a little."

"She scares me a little more than that, Milord, and only because she's a ghost. Come on." She gave Henry a nudge. "Let's open door one and see what lurks. If I remember right, it will be the only clean room of the bunch. Where better for a maid ghost than that, right?"

Henry nodded his agreement.

"Do you have a pocket watch, by chance? Not so certain I'm up for a discussion with Miss Pomeroy this evening, though it would be best now than when having Milord Priest present."

"No."

"Ah well." Para shrugged. "To the mystery, then. We'll take things as they come along and do our best by them. What say you?" Again he nodded as he followed her to the first door. "Why don't you have your bit of luck with this door? I checked it yesterday, but there's no telling what someone might have put on this particular door through the night."

Henry took to the task like a fish took to water, retrieving his tools from his pouch and whispering to himself quite cheerily as he went to work. Para stood over his shoulder, observing, and frowned in mild confusion when his actions didn't quite follow what she had done to achieve the same result. He didn't seem to move his tools more than just putting them into the keyhole. Then it was mostly a motion of the hands and the muttering.

Para crossed her arms in thoughtful consideration.

Straightening, Henry opened the door and then grinned up at her. "Just a little thing."

"Trap?"

He nodded and then entered the room, looking around with interest as he tucked his tools away. "This room is a mess!"

"What?" Para pushed wide the door, staring into the room with a blinking gaze. "Nefa's *ass*! This room was as near perfection as it could be yesterday!"

But true to Henry's report the bedding was thrown to the floor, the drawers of the dresser were emptied and upturned onto the bed, and the pictures previously on the wall were torn and broken. Someone had searched frantically for something, and they had more than likely found it, since she herself hadn't taken the time to search.

Para slapped her forehead and cursed her stupidity. So enthralled with the mystery of the noise in the basement, she hadn't seen the possibilities directly in front of her. "Bah!"

"What is it?"

"Of all the luck! Whatever they grabbed from here could have been mine, if I had rubbed two thoughts together."

Henry looked at the mess around him. "What could a maid have?"

"Well, she had a bit of something that someone wanted, by the looks of this. Maybe how she came to be a ghost? Maybe how her miss came to be one? Both? Neither? It doesn't matter, it's gone!" And that was the real rub.

"If she hid it well, it could still be here."

"Doubtful, but I guess it wouldn't hurt to have a look-see." She motioned to the far side. "You take a look over there and I'll paw through this mess. Shout out if you find a bit of something." *Like a bit of brain matter I lost somewhere....*

The search turned up nothing, causing Para to sink lower into her crankiness. Henry attempted to cheer her up, but even he opted to admit defeat after a while. As it approached the time of Miss Pomeroy's appearance, Para led him outside to the pond and fountain, determined to follow the miss to try and reason out the how and what, and possibly even the why and who, of her demise. She wasn't up to an actual conversation with the girl, and that mostly due to the fact that ghosts did such odd things!

It was hard to plan.

So, after she and Henry had hid as best they could, they waited for the girl's appearance while fighting off mild impatience. Para had less luck than Henry, who had retrieved his flute from his pouch and began sanding the corners to better smoothness before retrieving a knife and etching designs into the instrument. Para was left to the thoughts of the mystery as she absently retrieved her pipe from her inner pocket to bite down on the end. She couldn't even light it for fear that would draw undue attention.

As before, when Alicia Pomeroy appeared near the fountain, hovering over the water of the pond, she brought with her the haunting melody telling of a wandering girl and her search for home. Again, the song moved Para to a profound sense of pity for the girl. She had wandered for more than six months now, torn between life and death and tortured by the memories she had left behind. Her reaction to Derek proved that the memories were less than pleasant and goaded her to action outside of what she would normally have thought to do.

She felt a tug on her arm and shifted her attention to Henry beside her.

"What are we going to do?" he whispered. "Can I talk to her about her song?" he asked, holding up his flute.

"Not just yet, Milord Sidgwick. I'm not certain it would be the best thing to interrupt her. You wouldn't want her to eat you, would you?"

His eyes widened as he slowly shook his head.

"Then let's just take a turn behind her, shall we? Some say ghosts relive their last day. If that's the truth of the matter, then that should give us a peek into her bit of mystery. Right?"

Henry peeked around at Miss Pomeroy as she made her way gracefully from the pond to the brickwork path. Then he focused again on Para and nodded. "Where did she go yesterday?"

"She went to the stables and then the wood, and then was interrupted by Priest Derek." Para wondered if he had fully recovered from the shock. Setting the question aside, she scrutinized the route the ghost would take and plotted her and Henry's best course to follow without being seen.

"Will it take very long to follow her to these places? It's late and I'm getting hungry."

The thought and reference to food caused Para's stomach to growl. "I am sorry, Henry, but I've nothing but these little discs in my pocket. You'll need to wait until this adventure is over before you can have anything to eat. Unless you can find maid Marina and persuade her to get you something."

"Maybe there will be some berries in the woods," he said thoughtfully.

Para nudged him forward to the next place, hiding behind the railing of the front porch. They hurried with quiet steps and ducked behind the bushes there. The song continued without pause, letting them know that their presence was either not known, or Miss Pomeroy didn't regard them as a threat. *Poor Derek.* Being treated like that when he viewed the girl as an 'angel' in need of salvation… it was as cruel as life could be.

They shifted to their next point, on the other side of the front porch, and then the next and the next until they were outside the stable and she had begun her one-sided conversation with someone in one of the stalls. Para couldn't make out much more than she did the day before, so she sent the sylvan an inquiring gaze as she motioned into the stable.

Nodding, his expression shifted to that of intense listening while Para was left to attempt to pick out a word or three and make an entire conversation. It simply wasn't going to happen. When the conversation finished, she headed out to the corral where she stood for a long moment before turning back and exiting the stable, heading for the wood.

"So?" Para prompted in a hushed tone. "What was she going on about?"

"It didn't make much sense."

"But it was like a one-sided with another person?"

"Oh yes," Henry agreed, nodding. "I think she spoke with Lord Kensington."

"Cyruss?"

Henry grimaced. "No. Lord Kensington *senior*. She talked about Cyruss, though, saying that he was much closed and… separate."

"Hm. That's odd, to be talking about the son with the father. Well, perhaps not so odd if the father wanted to make certain she was following through. Bah…." She nudged Henry forward to the wood. "Come along again, Milord Sylvan. She's venturing deeper into the wood, and this is where we didn't follow yesterday."

The wood still gave her an ill feeling in the pit of her stomach.

Of course, so did the fact that Alicia had spoken with Lord Kensington about Cyruss the day of her disappearance. Something didn't fly quite right regarding that little bit of information. While she didn't think it of the father to do away with Miss Pomeroy – due to the fact that he had made the arrangements in the first place – there was something singularly wrong with her feeling free enough with him to discuss the object of the betrothal.

Frowning, Para rested a hand on Henry's shoulder to slow his pace along to the wood. "Are you sure she talked to Lord Kensington senior? What did she say that made you think that?"

Henry shrugged.

"Don't shrug at me with something as important as this," she complained. "We're trying to solve the mystery of a dead girl, and your little tidbit of information is going to lead us down a path — be it the wrong or right one is largely up to you at the moment."

"So dramatic," he grimaced.

"Deaths have a swing that direction, Milord Sylvan. Now, can you think again of what she said that made you think she talked to Kensington senior?" Para lifted her gaze from Henry's somewhat annoyed countenance to check on the location of their subject; she had paused just outside the boundaries of the wood.

"I told you it didn't make any sense."

"Aye, you did at that, but there must have been something. She certainly seemed a bit too cheerily carrying on with her side of things for— Didn't she say a name at all?"

"No. She only said that her impression of Cyruss was what I told you. Then she said that there wasn't another way or else her father would have done that."

Another way… another way…. Para's mind wrestled with a few possibilities for those who would care one way or the other if there was another way to the situation Miss Pomeroy had found herself. *Marina, maybe, since she came to be so fond….* Her eyes narrowed and she gave Henry's shoulder a grip to urge him forward again.

"It has to be Derek," she grumbled. Who else would have proposed 'another way'? *But didn't he know that Cyruss had refused the match to their father? But when?* And was it before this particular conversation? This, of course, did nothing to help build his credibility as an innocent bystander. His tendency toward compassion and helping others was sending him right to the gallows. Para swore, slapping an imaginary cap against the thigh of her breeches.

If Para's venture into the wood had been anything other than the search for clues to solve a murder mystery, she very likely would have enjoyed the sights and smells. The aroma of the evergreens tingled her nostrils with their spicy tang, this softened by the fragrance of the flora and fauna after the misty drizzle that afternoon. The mixture of the two together was the epitome of nature; something a ranger had the fortune of smelling most of their life. It would have reminded her of better days when peace was the daily adventure on her way to the next town. Today, unfortunately, it was paired with the mysterious disappearance of a fifteen year old girl who had deserved something a lot more fulfilling.

In fact, the fragrance began to set Para into one of her infamous foul moods.

She pulled Henry down into a crouch as Miss Pomeroy approached a vine encrusted gazebo with a failing roof. She ascended the few stairs, pausing in the center of the decrepit building for a long collection of minutes before kneeling, her expression showing the intensity of one who gathered something of importance. Para craned her neck to try and catch the sight of where it was hidden and noted a bench that wasn't the usual marble.

"There's a bit of a secret hiding place here, Henry," she whispered. She hoped for Derek's sake that it shed some light in a different direction than at his feet. Shifting her focus to the sylvan at her side, she made a slight motion toward the gazebo. "When she's done with this bit of remembering, I want you to follow after her – not letting her see you of course – and meet me back at the fountain."

Henry nodded.

"Don't let anyone else see you either. There's some nonsense going on in the basement that we've not had a chance to take a look at. The last thing you want is to be caught up in that bit of madness, especially if it has anything to do with the experiment room on the second floor. Wouldn't they love to get their paws on you!" It wasn't too much to believe that Henry would have heard worse stories than she had of those arcanists and sorcerers that used the elf people as a subject of experimentation.

Magic users had a leaning toward eccentricity, and their access to power did nothing to help matters.

Grimacing, Para retrieved her pipe from the pocket of her vest, the action bringing Munwar to mind. If he found anything of use about the elder Kensington, she swore she would kiss the stoic warrior right on the lips. It grew old to have everything point to the priest as the only suspect, to say nothing of how that went so hard against what she thought of the man. Her instinct about people was more right than wrong, and to be so wrong about a priest when he was one of the first that she trusted in the first place? No, it didn't do much for her confidence at the moment, and the last thing she needed was a reason to second guess every decision.

Especially not in her line of work.

Para's ears focused on the soft sound of weeping, dragging her back to the duty at hand and sending her attention to the gazebo. The girl's willowy form leaned against one of the rotting support posts, her forehead pressed against her hands. Para lowered her gaze to the still unlit pipe between her fingers and blinked back the slight burning in her eyes.

"Are all ghosts sad?" Henry asked in a soft voice.

"No, Henry. Not all." At least not as distraught as Alicia Pomeroy seemed.

Alicia wept for what seemed a long time before she offered herself several encouragements and then a scolding for allowing the childish tears. "It will be all right," she assured in a voice as beautiful as her song. "Look to the sunrise and there will be hope."

Then she smoothed the flowing layers of her dress, wiped the moisture from her face, and lifted her chin as she stepped down from the gazebo to journey back toward the palace. Henry sent a sidelong glance to Para, who continued to stare after the girl in guarded contemplation. With a shrug, he followed stealthily after the ghost.

'Look to the sunrise and there will be hope.' Para lowered her gaze to the grass at her feet, looping her thumbs on the belt of her scabbard. How did such a girl come to be used as a peace-maker in a feud? It rang much like leading a lamb to the slaughter, or to the lair of a lion.

"Nefa's bones," she grumbled.

She heaved a sigh and gave a shake of her head before heading toward the gazebo. There she saw the carved wooden bench in place of the usual marble often seen in a gazebo such as this. Kneeling, she searched the right support for the catch—a book-sized door popped open on the side, revealing a leather-bound journal.

The book had seen a lot of use, or so told the worn leather cover. Para smoothed the cobwebs from the cubby, feeling guilty as she did so for planning to read the girl's private thoughts. "My apologies, Milady," Para said as she retrieved the book, "but I think this will help find a few answers." All she could do was hope they were the right ones.

She opened the journal to the last page, dated nearly seven months ago.

I am a foolish girl for I, Alicia Elizabeth Marie Pomeroy, have fallen in love. Why is such an admirable occasion 'foolish', you ask? Because I have fallen in love – and not idly, mind you! With my whole heart! With my entire soul and with each breath in my lungs do I love him! – I have fallen in love with the younger brother of my betrothed. The even more foolish of all the foolish actions I could have done being that he is a priest, devoted to his god and the teachings he has studied so diligently for so many years, and forbidden to marry.

But will this cease the beat of my heart for him? Surely do I say 'nay'! What would my love be if such a forbidding rent it from me? So I tell thee 'nay' again. I will continue to love him until the end of my days; even after, if the gods allow. And yes, I shall marry his brother, for then I will be ever close to him, by his side and his heart, even should he never know of my adoration.

Para swore as she slammed the journal closed, only just able to prevent the action from throwing it clear. The girl's life seemed to have been cursed since the first day she had been introduced to the Kensington name. The question now would be if Cyruss had found out about the girl's feelings for his brother. If so, would he have retaliated against her if he didn't care for her one way or the other?

She tucked the journal back into its hiding place, replacing the locked panel as snugly as before. Then she straightened, as if she carried a weight upon her shoulders, and turned back for the palace and the mystery that waited on yonder hill.

'Look to the sunrise and there will be hope.'

Alicia Pomeroy hadn't lived to see the sunrise, so did that mean her hope still waited?

"Bah! Para Sedi, you get yourself in hand and solve this mystery without all the dramatics," she scolded fiercely. "The girl deser—" A shrill scream pierced the air, and that cut short by a sharp crash and splash. Para bolted forward, darting through the wood and then sprinting for the pond and fountain. She made out Henry's small form at the balcony railing and then shifted her focus to the red water of the fountain, that foreboding color slowly receding into itself and then vanishing altogether.

Scowling, she kicked a stone at the fountain and let loose a collection of expletives that voiced her displeasure, disgust, irritation, annoyance, and rage at the entire situation. Never had a mystery set her so much on edge as this one, and she wasn't so certain that she cared for the feeling battling inside. In fact, if it hadn't been for the fact she had given Lord Pomeroy her word, she could have been tempted to walk away from the entire situation altogether. If only to regain her calm! But her word had been given, and she was always one to follow through with that.

She pointed at the fountain and warned, "You're next, or by Nefa's blood I'll eat my pipe!" What she meant she wasn't certain. But at that moment the threat made her feel better, and that was all that mattered. The sylvan figure on the balcony drew her glare. "What in blazes happened?"

"Someone pushed her!"

"What?" Para nearly shot the question like one of her arrows. "Who, Henry?" and she asked that question at a near shrill pitch. The suspense began to take its toll. "Who pushed her?"

"It was too dark. All I could see was his back."

"For the love of—" Her lips whitened as she pressed them into a thin line. "All right," she said with forced calm. "At least tell me what happened leading up to the push."

"She sat at her vanity brushing her hair. Then the door to her room opened, but she didn't notice at first. I guess she saw their reflection because she turned and stood. Then all of a sudden she looked frightened and started backing away... and then he pushed her!"

"And you didn't see his face when he turned to leave?" she asked, incredulous.

Henry splayed his hands out. "He vanished!"

Para slapped her forehead. "I can't have a single coin here, can I?" She threw up her hands. "Fine. I'm done." At least for that day, she was. She turned and stalked back toward town, ignoring Henry's squawk of protest as he shimmied down one of the balcony support posts and scurried after her.

Nona King | 135

Eleven

"Why can't we tell him?"

Para's brows descended as she regarded the sylvan sitting at the table across from her in the common room of the inn, the *Journeyman's Palace*. "Because it's our little secret, that's why, Henry. Don't you like keeping secrets?"

He wrinkled his nose. "But this isn't really a secret all that fun to keep, Para. It would be better if we had found some gold in that old gazebo. That would be a secret!"

"Aye, now that would be a secret worth keeping, but let's keep this one just the same. All right? You know how Munwar frets over little things. He might fret over something, and we don't want that big wall upset, do we?"

Henry regarded Para with a slight tilt of head as his eyes took on a thoughtful expression. Then he grinned. "You weren't supposed to go to the palace by yourself!" he squealed, pointing. "That's a secret! That's a secret!"

"For the— Henry, I swear if you don't stop your caterwauling, I will put you outside an arcanist's door and have him make sport of you."

The sylvan continued to laugh, holding his sides and nearly tipping backwards off the bench.

Frowning, Para decided against pressing further. She

seemed to be an endless source of delight and amusement to the little shrub, and she wasn't so certain that it settled well at the moment. Mun hadn't ordered her to stay clear of the palace; he knew better than to order her to do *anything*. On the down side, she knew it hadn't been one of the brightest ideas to head up to yonder hill with only a shrub as company....

A shadowy form in the farthest corner of the inn continued to gather Para's attention, shifting her eye from all other focuses every few minutes. There didn't seem to be anything familiar about him, and Para wasn't so certain he was a bad character. He only continued to gather her attention.

Para drew her pipe from one pouch and a deck of cards from the other. "How about a game, Milord Sidgwick? Loser pays the tab."

Henry's lower lip protruded as he frowned down at the deck of cards, his hands folded as they rest on the table. "Cards? I don't like playing cards with you."

"It's just a friendly game, Milord. Come along. Be a sport." She shuffled the cards with one hand as she lit her pipe with the other, regarding the shadowed form in the corner while seemingly watching the sylvan.

He was a tall man, by the breadth of his shoulders and how he loomed over the others at the table; somewhat dark in complexion; haggard also. He wore chainmail under his green tunic, and a worn leather scabbard at his hip in which was sheathed a bastard sword of exceptional quality.

"Come along," she said again, restraining a reaction when the shadowed form stood. "Just one hand."

Henry crossed his arms and turned his face away. "No. I don't want to play cards with you." Then he took his flute from his pouch and slipped down from the bench. "I'm going to go play my flute outside," he informed, and didn't waste a moment exiting the premises.

Para thoughtfully stared after him as she puffed on her pipe, wondering again about the little shrub and just what he was—other than a sylvan with an interesting knack for removing traps and locks from doors.

"Might I have a word with you outside?"

The voice behind her was deep and coarse, and when she turned she had to tip her head back to look up into the cold brown eyes of someone who looked eerily familiar. "Cyruss Kensington, I take it?"

"A word, Ranger?" Cyruss Kensington prompted again.

Para kept her seat, offering to the bench across from her. "You can string as many words together as you would like, Milord. Have a seat and I'll order you ale to start the conversation." She noted the rank insignia on the helmet held under his arm. "General, you won't get me outside this room, so you may as well enjoy the ale and the bench beneath you."

The request rankled him, Para noticed, but she refused to step one foot outside of where she felt the safest. And here, where she knew Lord Pomeroy held sway, was where she currently felt the safest. So, here she would stay—especially since Munwar and Derek were expected soon.

After motioning to the barkeep for a pair of ales, she took a long draught on her pipe. "What can I do for you, General?"

"It has come to my attention that you are seeking answers regarding Alicia Pomeroy's disappearance." He slowly lowered himself onto the bench across from her, setting his helmet onto the table between them.

"Aye. Have anything to offer in that respect?"

"Nothing more than what you have already discovered."

I bet. She gestured toward him with her pipe. "Then what can I do for you?" she asked again.

He regarded her with a stony gaze that rivaled Mun's most intimidating expression, his hands balled into fists as he glowered

Nona King | 139

at her from across the table. "Cease this investigation. It will reveal nothing of value and only continues to strain an already tenuous relationship between families."

"It seems to me, Milord General, that the feeling between your two families is where it's at because of Miss Alicia taking a turn over the side. Your marriage to the Lady Andonia of Arielle hasn't helped anything over to rights, I'm willing to bet."

"My marriage is none of your business, Ranger."

"That may well be, but the arrangement between you and Miss Pomeroy is what I'm getting at, Milord. That is what I'll keep at until I find one of two things: Her body, or the one that pushed her over the balcony. Actually, I'm out to find both in hopes to set the poor girl to rest." Para suddenly leaned forward. "Don't you wish her peace, General?"

General Cyruss Kensington tightened his jaw, the leather of his gloved hands creaking in protest. "I wish she and her kind had never come to our family seat, for with them has come nothing but challenges and conflicts. She, who was offered as a maker of peace, has wrought everything to the contrary. Do I wish her peace?" He scoffed and stood in a clamor of chain and leather. "Inform Lord Pomeroy that any further trespassing onto our lands will incur the wrath of me and my armies." With that, he exited the inn.

Para stared after him, her eyes narrowed and her fingers toying with the end of her pipe as she tapped a rhythm on the metal of her ale pint. She didn't know for certain if the man was a cold-hearted bastard because he was a murderer, or because he had been in the military far too many years to remember how to be civil.

She still glowered at the front entrance when Mun and Derek entered. Her expression lightened and she stood, lifting her pint to their safe return. "Milords! Welcome and good evening! Ale for everyone!"

A cheer rumbled through the common room and very nearly brought down the roof.

Motioning to the seats around the table, she urged them both to sit. "You must be thirsty! Here are your ales, now come and tell us the tale of your journey!" She straddled her chair and puffed her pipe as she took in the tired look to their eyes.

"We were unable to meet with the elder Kensington," Mun informed, pulling the leather gauntlets from his hands. "However, Lord Kensington senior confirmed all that we have been told of the refusal and the reluctance on the part of the elder Kensington."

He must have had scouts along the way to message him on any approaching from here. Yet why would he feel the need to make such an effort if he wasn't at all responsible for her disappearance? Why would he distance himself from direct questioning in front of his father?

Para noticed Derek's downcast face and motioned toward him with her pipe. "What say you, Milord Derek?"

The priest pushed away the ale as he stood. "My apologies, but I am unwell. I will meet with you in the morning. Good evening." He left the inn without another word.

Para's eyebrows twitched upward and she focused a questioning gaze on Mun. "What ails our resident priest?"

"His brother recently married a lady of wealth and rank equaling that of the Kensington family."

"Ah. Didn't get the approval of the others, did he?"

"No."

"Doesn't say much for him taking to the arrangement with the Pomeroys, does it, Mun?"

"Indeed, it does not."

"Derek did not say much on the way back?"

Mun shook his head before taking a healthy draught of his ale. "He is mightily troubled by the actions of his brother, Par.

With the haunting of Miss Alicia, he suffers a daily torture."

She absently nodded, staring down at the softly glowing embers of her pipe. "I went to the palace today."

The warrior pressed his lips into a thin line.

"Followed the girl along her rounds and found a bit of new information." She met Mun's gaze. "The girl was mightily in love with the priest, which I'm thinking is one of the things that keep her here: She doesn't want to be apart from him."

Mun heaved a sigh as he lowered his eyes to a scrutiny of the froth of his ale.

"And, Henry came along for this bit of adventure. He saw her ghostly visage get pushed from the balcony to the fountain. Henry couldn't see the bastard who did the deed – shame – but I'm still of the mind it wasn't our lord priest."

Mun nodded. "His character is the direct opposite to the violence of death."

"I couldn't have said it better, Mun."

"What do you propose for the morrow?"

"Get into that dungeon, and post Henry in the girl's room to see about getting a face for the silhouette. You, I and the priest should be able to take on whatever has made the basement home. Although, it would be nice to have the extra fingers along."

"Perhaps if we take him to the lower levels, the mystery of the silhouette will solve itself?" Mun offered.

"Aye, there is that." She tapped the dregs from the pipe cup and tucked it away. "Cyruss was here just before you arrived."

Mun's grip on the pint of ale tightened, causing a slight slosh. "Indeed?"

"Aye, and he's told me to tell Lord Pomeroy that any other feet on their property earns a bit of rough treatment."

"Hm. Odd that." He regarded Para's intense scrutiny out the window toward the Kensington hill. "First light?"

"Aye."

Twelve

Para stowed the last of the rations into her pack. "So it's agreed?"

Mun nodded as he slung his pack across his broad frame. "We will notify Lord Pomeroy of our challenge with General Kensington so he can be ready for any retaliation."

"And then we head up to the palace," Henry said, and he continued to check the contents of his numerous pouches.

She sent a glance toward Derek, who continued to stare down at the flooring of her room while fingering the holy symbol that dangled from the cord at the waist of his tunic. "Derek?"

He lifted his gaze. "Pardon?"

Smiling, she motioned toward him. "Your role is what?"

"Ah. My apologies. I am responsible for turning aside any possible attack from my brother's soldiers. We are only to battle them if they refuse to relent."

Para gave a curt nod. "All right, everyone, I believe we're ready for this little bit of adventure." She heaved her pack onto her back and then gestured ahead. "Forward march."

As they strolled purposefully through the town of Pomeroy it seemed they were watched with a somewhat guarded view by those few townspeople that milled the streets at first light—mostly fisher folk and trades people. It was as if the General had slipped scouts and spies into the populace to begin planting rumors and irritants that might urge the party on their way from town. Either that or the townspeople had an uncanny knack to know when something was amiss. From Para's experience traveling, she wouldn't discount either as a possibility. Ghosts weren't the only people that acted oddly.

Mun brought up the front, Henry and Derek in the center, and Para the rear so that she could make certain that all coin purses stayed in the appropriate pockets. Due to the aforementioned guarded attitude from the people, though, they didn't have any issues with sticky fingers. In fact, those tradesmen in their path veered one way or the other when the troupe approached. Yes, it made the going easy, but this added to Para's sense that something wasn't quite right.

The sylvan also seemed to notice something amiss. Para continued to catch him sending glances to the different market fronts as if he sought out a specific cause of suspicion. When Para also began to scrutinize the windows and doors, she noted a lot of closed shutters and drawn drapes shutting out any view of the streets below.

That didn't settle very well at all, as it made Para think that no one wanted to be a witness to some type of atrocity—such as an army coming to slaughter a group of four innocent individuals only doing their best to solve the mystery of a girl's disappearance. It sent Para's temper soaring and caused her to take a mental tally of the daggers in boot, glove and vest. *No, not enough to fend off an army,* she mused with a frown.

It was too bad she didn't know how to utter the incantation to plant a well timed delayed-blast fireball in the midst of the invading force, if and when it came.

The usual maid answered the door, her expression registering surprise at the four of them on her doorstep. But then she calmed herself and ushered them inside and to the side parlor, taking orders for tea or another hot drink to help fight off the biting cold of the early morning breeze. All refused anything to eat or drink, and they remained standing as the maid went in search of Lord Pomeroy upon Para's request. She wasn't certain yet how she was going to tell the lord that his mansion could very well fall under attack, but she knew that however she decided to tell him wouldn't go over.

"Para," Derek spoke up, "I will tell him of our attention and the possible result. It is my brother who is the cause of the distress."

"Brothers or not, I accepted this adventure and so I will be the one to take responsibility of whatever needs to be told and whom it needs to be told to. You, Milord Priest, have enough expectation on your plate with the duty of turning back the soldiers." He would also be the only one able to do anything for Miss Pomeroy's body if and when they found her... unless Henry happened to have a wand of resurrection in one of his belt pouches.

Lord Pomeroy appeared several minutes later dressed in a house robe and slippers, his hair disheveled and sleep still evident in his eyes and expression. There was even the crease of a pillow marring his face.

"My, but isn't this a collection of adventurers?" he mused in a still sleepy tone. He cleared his throat several times as he gestured to the chairs and couches around the parlor. "Please. Sit. What can I do for you?"

"No seats, thank you, Milord," Para said, shaking her head. "We wanted to let you know of a little stick in the pudding that might come about from our early hour jaunt to the palace. General Kensington isn't too keen on continuing the questions, so we're not welcome to the palace after yesterday."

"He threatened harm to you?"

"Of a sort. He said another trespass would make him send

out his armies."

Lord Pomeroy lowered himself into the chair in shocked silence, his hand groping behind him for the arm of the chair to steady him.

"If you don't want to deal with the soldiers or the Kensingtons, I suggest you bug on out of here for a time, Milord. Leave word at *The Journeyman's Palace* of where you're off to, and we'll seek you out once the mystery is done. There's no need for you to get caught up in this foolishness."

"Why would he do such a thing?" Lord Pomeroy asked, and his tone sounded perplexed. "My only daughter has vanished while under the protection of his roof. Am I not justified to seek resolve? He has offered nothing by way of resolution, so I have had need to seek it out myself!"

Para nodded. "Aye, that be true, Milord, but he's done with the seeking and wants whatever secrets lie on yonder hill to remain there. You and I have another want, and that is what I and these others are on our way to do. Because you hired us, true, but also because Miss Alicia deserves this bit of answering. We're set. We're off, by your leave."

Lord Pomeroy stared at them with wide eyes for a collection of long moments before lowering his gaze and giving them a slight incline of head.

The group bowed and showed themselves out, pausing on the doorstep to gauge their surroundings and any possible danger before heading with purpose toward the Kensington palace. Para felt for the lord. He was stuck between two boulders that, if moved, would start a rock slide. She hoped that whatever solve they found to the mystery would lessen the danger he found himself in, but she knew that he was the type that would have sacrificed his peace for the restful slumber of his missing daughter.

Odd that you're suddenly calling her missing and not dead, Par, she mused. It was, but she didn't want to invest the time in the wondering of why.

"He has been wronged greatly by my brother," Derek offered in a low and intense voice.

She shifted her focus to him as he walked at her side. "Aye, Milord Priest. Keep that in mind when you offer to make amends for whatever we discover on yonder hill. Anything done by your brother is his to collect the debt on, or your father as head of the house."

"But they are my kin."

"Aye, there is that. But who of them all has stuck his neck out to try and repair what's been done? You, Milord, and you very nearly had your head handed back because of it."

"But Miss Pomeroy… she…."

Para rested a hand on his shoulder. "Derek, let tomorrow keep itself. Right now we've got a basement to search out, so we'll need your focus in the here and now."

Derek clenched his jaw, holding her gaze for a long moment before inclining his head to the affirmative and shifting his focus to the palace. "I hope she knows that had I realized this was to be her future, I would have stopped the alliance."

"Aye, Milord Derek. I'm sure she does." She gave his shoulder a firm grip and then motioned ahead. "Go ask the little shrub to play us a lively tune on that whistle of his. We all of us need a bit of pepper in our step."

With a nod, Derek stepped forward to Henry's side to make the request. The sylvan's expression lit up like a star, and the tune he chose to play for them had their spirits rising like the mist from a meadow. If there was one thing the Sylvans knew, it was music.

Para, on the other hand, continued to be troubled. The elder Kensington brother didn't seem to care one way or the other that his actions made him look even more the guilty party.

Even Derek thought so—no, he hadn't admitted that fact, but what else would have bothered the priest to this extent? *Could the General be innocent?* But who else had the reason to slaughter the guards and, according to the ghost Alicia's re-enactment, push her over the balcony to her death?

Frowning, Para retrieved a smooth stone from the road and chucked it far into the distance. It ricocheted off the roof of a house and caused a complaining roar from an alley cat on the other side. Para smirked, but that quickly faded when she lifted her gaze to the Kensington palace beyond. At this point it wouldn't surprise her one bit if Lord Kensington senior had killed the girl so that the families would continue to battle. Money could be best gained during war, and hadn't the Kensingtons gained power over the surrounding cities without the help of a Pomeroy-Kensington alliance?

She gave a shiver.

"Par."

Mun's somber tone gathered her focus. He directed that focus to the main gate leading up to the palace. Four guards bearing the Kensington family crest stood two deep, the gates closed and secured.

"Ah. So it's to be like that, is it now?" The four halted, and Para came to stand next to Derek. "Milord Priest, now is when your use of your family name comes into play."

An expression of determination hardened his features as he straightened and stepped forward. It was at that moment he could have been his elder brother's twin. Even the guards, likely set by the General himself, were impressed by the younger Kensington's strength of purpose as he strode toward them. She could see it in their eyes and the way they shuffled their feet at his approach.

"This might work after all," she admitted under her breath.

Mun sent her a glance, and Henry snickered.

"You, there! Open the gate immediately," Derek ordered.

"We've been ordered to open the gate for no one," one of them reported, and he cast a shifty glance to his compatriots.

"And I've ordered you to open it," the priest countered, his brow furrowed with a somewhat dangerous expression of irritation. "Do you not know who I am? I'm Lord Kensington, the younger."

The soldier sent the other guards another glance. "That may be, Milord, but the General—"

"Are you disobeying an order, soldier?" He motioned roughly to the palace. "I have business in the palace and will not be delayed. Open the door immediately or I will have you put in the dungeons."

The guard couldn't hold Derek's gaze, and when the priest took a threatening step forward, the guards flinched and turned to set to the task of unlocking and opening the gate. Para could have kissed the priest with how well he set the guards on their ear.

The four passed without a glance, no point in tempting the fates, and then listened in amusement as Derek ordered the guards to seal up the gate yet again and go about their duty as previously ordered. It was a touch of genius is what it was, and she couldn't have done better herself.

"The threat was a nice touch," she offered the priest as an aside.

"It wasn't too much? Perhaps I should have reasoned with them instead?" he asked, and she could see the thoughtful concern on his expression.

And they think this priest killed the girl? Para restrained a scoff.

"They are military, Milord Priest," Mun offered. "You must understand their life of discipline and immediate action, being raised in such close proximity to your brother?"

"I suppose."

Nona King | 149

Mun gripped the priest's shoulder as they continued toward the palace. "It was well done, Milord."

Derek's ears reddened as he offered his thanks.

"Don't be sure that there won't be another soldier group or two in the palace itself," Para reminded, motioning ahead. "The General put those soldiers there for no other reason than to keep us off of yonder hill, and there's no reason to think he doesn't have a few more along the way. He only doesn't know that his own brother is helping us. Or he does but doesn't think Milord Priest presents much of a challenge."

Mun glanced toward the priest, as did Henry, but the priest didn't react to her statement of fact. Para noticed that with a slight arch to her right eyebrow. It had her wondering to the type of relationship the brothers shared, if any at all. Conflict was the norm between siblings, she supposed, especially those so different in character. But there was still something that seemed off kilter, though she couldn't put her finger on what it could be. An irritation, to say the least.

"Uh oh…."

This time it was Henry who commented, drawing Para's focus from her scrutiny of the priest to the front entry ahead. As at the gate, there were four soldiers set to the duty of guarding it against trespassers. These four gave the immediate impression of trouble, and Para had a feeling that neither persuasion nor brusqueness would get them past.

"Heads up," she warned in a low tone, her hand resting on the pommel of her long sword.

Mun shrugged his shoulders in his usual act of unlocking his claymore from the sheath on his back. Henry reached into one of his pouches while Para heard Derek begin and finish a chant of blessing over the group. All in all, Para felt a swell of pride at how well the group reacted together to her simple warning.

One of the soldiers stepped forward. "You need to exit the

grounds immediately," he informed in a hard tone, gesturing back the way they had come.

Derek stepped forward a ways from the other three. "I'm Lord Kensington, the younger, and have business in the palace. Stand aside."

The soldiers bowed but didn't alter their position. "Lord Kensington, you need to exit the grounds immediately upon the order of your brother, General Kensington."

The priest sent Para a sidelong glance. "My brother does not hold sway over my comings and goings, soldier, nor is he the sole lord and master over this estate," he said with admiral intensity. "If you wish to send two of your men along with us as we go about our business beyond the doors, by all means. Regardless, we are entering this palace."

Para minutely frowned. Having two tag-a-longs would be an irritant, to be certain. She would rather fight them all and leave their bleeding bodies on the steps. It was nothing less than what they deserved for running with an ass like General Kensington.

"Milord," the soldier said, "don't be foolish. We will not leave our post, just as we will not allow you to enter. Return with word of the General's permission and we will stand aside. Not before."

The priest opened his mouth to respond, but Para stepped forward, her arm outstretched across Derek's chest directing his focus to her serious expression. "Milord, might I have a word?"

"By all means." He stepped back.

Para gave a nod of thanks before shifting her attention to the soldiers, her hands resting easily on both the pommel of her long sword and her opposite hip. She presented a picture of ease, like a lioness just before she lunged. "Gentlemen, allow me to introduce myself."

She heard the ring of metal as Mun unsheathed the glowing vision of his father's claymore. The soldiers crouched, their hands tightening on their pole-arms as she pulled free her long sword and lunged in one flowing movement. Deflecting the pole-arm, she struck at his shoulder with the dagger in her other hand, leaving it and palming another as she disarmed him with the continued circle of her long sword.

She brought the second dagger to his throat.

"Give the word to stand down, Milord," she said in a low voice, eyes narrowed, "and you live."

Gripping the bleeding mess of his left shoulder around the still submerged blade of the dagger, he glowered down at her for a moment before uttering a sharp command to his men—still motionless behind him. They dropped their weapons, which Derek and Henry quickly gathered up.

"Mun, would you mind opening the door?" She didn't look from the soldier's gaze.

Mun complied, shoving the other guards deeper into the early morning chill of the palace. Henry closed the door and immediately set to the duty of lighting the nearest candelabrum to shed some much needed light.

"Milords, we've a special place in mind for you four while we go about our business. Come this way please." She retrieved her dagger from the man's shoulder while ignoring his shout of complaint. "Derek, would you please heal this man?"

As Derek set to the healing, Mun and Henry led the other three guards through the parlor and study to the previously found secret treasure room. Once the man's wound had stopped bleeding, she led him also to the room, pushing him inside rather roughly before closing the secret door.

She sheathed her sword. "Milord Sidgwick, if you could please seal this up to keep them out of the way?"

Nodding, Henry hurried forward and did as requested, locking the secret door so that it could only be unlocked and opened from the outside.

"Aye, that has it. Now, shall we be about our business?" she asked as she wiped the blood from her dagger.

"Should we finish our search of the second floor?" Mun asked.

"Eh. I'm more curious to know what's below. We couldn't find a trigger to the fountain." Para shrugged. "She starts and ends at that fountain, which has me by the head. If there isn't a secret door there, then maybe it's just… well, maybe she's under it?" She shrugged again.

Mun inclined his head in thoughtful silence.

"I don't know of any secret passage beneath the fountain," Derek offered, "but I suppose that doesn't mean there couldn't have been something added."

"Aye." Para urged everyone out of the study to the dining hall beyond. "Come along then everyone. We've a lot of ground to cover, and bleating like a herd of goats won't get it done."

Mun smirked. "Impatience is only a virtue when adventuring," he offered as an aside to Henry.

Henry sniggered.

Once the group arrived in the laundry room beyond the kitchen, they paused for several moments. Para had it in her mind to catch sound of the basement residents before she set foot on the first step. The only problem being that the residents didn't cooperate with her timing. Disgusted, Para assigned Henry as first string.

He eagerly took to the opportunity, the awareness and intensity glittering in his eyes as he sought to determine if the way was plagued with traps. He found a trap consisting of a poisoned dart at about the third step down, which he disarmed and saved, tucking it into a compartment in one of his belt pouches. That was the odd thing about thieves, Para observed. They had a fetish for saving things of that sort and using them later.

The habit saved coin, if nothing else.

Unfortunately, Henry missed a trip wire on the fifth step, which Derek had the misfortune of finding. It sent him careening down at least four steps, nearly colliding into Henry. Mun was able to catch him by the back of his tunic and keep him from sending them all to their deaths at the foot of the steps.

Derek's ears and face reddened, and Para hadn't heard anyone apologize more profusely than the priest did after. They all tried to reassure him that everyone had a similar issue at least once in their adventuring lifetime, but the man still beat himself for not paying attention to his own step.

That disaster averted, the group continued cautiously on. Mun and Para lit the torches found at the base of the stairs, saving their lanterns for a later time. No one knew how complex the basement corridors and rooms would be, and so they knew it would be best to reserve as much of their light as possible for a greater necessity.

Henry continued at point, Para directly behind him, and they both searched the walls and floors for more traps and surprises. She knew it would be slow going, that being the motivation for starting the search at first light, just as she knew that they would very likely have company from above at some point. Such was the reason Mun had volunteered to take up the rear of the procession.

"Is it always this slow going?" Derek whispered.

"No, Milord. Not always. If we hadn't found those traps on the stair, I would have let Henry off the hook."

Derek inclined his head in thoughtful silence.

"The theory being that if they don't care to protect the entry into a place like this, there very likely isn't a reason they should set traps further in. A good adventurer keeps his eye out one way or the other, mostly at doors, but not at this crawling pace for the rest of the place." She sent the priest a sidelong glance. "Have somewhere to be?"

The priest smiled. "No, Mil—Para. Curiosity, I'm afraid. Not having been in a situation such as this before, I find myself overrun with questions."

"Questions are good. They could keep you alive once you start adventuring."

He blinked. "You believe I should begin adventuring?"

"Why not? You reacted well atop with those soldiers, that blessing coming in handy at just the right time. I'm willing to wager you would take to the adventure much like me or Munwar there."

Derek's eyebrow twitched upward as he regarded her with a thoughtful expression. "You have given me a thought to ponder. Thank you."

Her green eyes twinkled in amusement. "Glad to be of service, Milord. Now I believe Henry's beckoning. I better attend the shrub before he sheds a leaf."

Henry glowered at her. "Stop calling me a shrub!"

"Aye, aye, Milord Sylvan." She crouched down to scrutinize the flagstone Henry indicated. "What have you found?"

"I don't know. I don't think it's a trap, but…." He shrugged as he stared down at the flagstone, which seemed much like every other stone.

"Want me to have a gander, do you?" She adjusted her position to one more comfortable for a closer scrutiny, and retrieved her own tools as she eyed the flagstone. "All right, you there," she muttered under her breath, "Let's have your secret, shall we? We're all friends here…." Para blew into the cracks and crevices of the flagstone's edges, bringing forth a small brush to perform a further investigation of a slightly raised corner. "Aye, that's the way. What have you here?"

Shifting to lying on her stomach, she brought her face down until her cheek pressed against the other flagstone so she could peer into the slight crack. Then she palmed a slim tool and pushed it inside—there was a click and a bit of wall pulled back from the wall immediately to their right.

She sat up as everyone shifted their position, staring wide-eyed into the small alcove and the scroll perched quite securely on a granite pedestal.

Thirteen

"Nefa's bright and shiny—!" Para bolted to her feet and was in the alcove in less than a stride, her eyes alight with excitement. "An arcanist's scroll! Do you have any idea how much they will pay for something like this?"

Mun gave a slight shake of his head, his lips twitching upward.

"Why?" Derek asked, unaware of the warrior's silent amusement.

"Because, more often than not, it has a higher level spell than what they have." Para put aside her tool as she began scrutinizing the pedestal. "Milord Sidgwick, can you help me take a look for traps guarding this little treasure?"

Henry stood to his feet after expending a great sigh for such a small body. He ambled over to the alcove. "Para, we don't need a smelly old scroll," he complained.

"You might not need it, but I'm taking it along with us just the same. Knowledge like this is priceless to the Arcanist Guild!" She finished her scrutiny and then snatched up the scroll, removing the leather strip and unfurling— "What the blazes? It's blank?" Para hissed her disappointment as she tucked the scroll into her side bag.

"Is the parchment itself worth coin?" Derek asked.

Nona King | 157

"Oh, a few coppers maybe, but with this scroll being hidden away such as it was, I'm of the mind that I'd like to take a better look at it once we're out of this mess. Something itches at my head that someone only wants us to think it's blank."

"Has that happened in the past?"

Para urged Henry to continue with his trap scouting and then focused on the priest. "No, I can't say as it has, but it just strikes me as odd. Doesn't it you?"

"I wouldn't have thought anything of it, to be truthful," he admitted with a slight pinking to his ears.

"Well, now you might down the road, and it may just give you a pouch full of coin."

He smiled, but any response was cut short by a gesture from Henry that elicited a warning hiss from Mun and sent them all back against the wall. After the initial scurry to the side, Para crept nimbly to Mun's side and sent him an inquiring glance. He made a motion around the corner that indicated voices to have been heard, and that being of at least two individuals.

Para peeked around Mun's towering frame to notice Henry busily setting a trap using the poison dart he had just picked up at the stairs. She smirked and elbowed Derek, urging him to peer over her shoulder and see for himself. His eyebrows twitched upward in surprise and then he smiled at her with a nod of acknowledgement.

If the dart ended up being a fast acting poison, they would only need to take care of one resident, unless there were more in the party and only two were talkative. Things stranger than that had happened to Mun and her in the past. In fact, she remembered one time they had been surprised to find a group of eight around the corner when the conversation had only hinted at three. It had been an interesting battle, to say the least, and both Mun and Para had opted to run for a distance to regroup before facing off the remaining. Looking back, she was glad they had only been bandits and not trained military, such as what could be the case now.

"He makes me afraid to sleep at night," one of the men said to the other.

"He does at that. I don't think I've slept a full night's sleep for the past two months," grumbled another.

"Two months nothing! I haven't slept more than two hours at a time for the last six. Death would be better than this bit, I'm telling you!"

Well, gents, we'll be happy to oblige... once you step around this corner and have a look at what's waiting on the other side. It was then they triggered the poison dart, causing a shout and then immediate groan and crash as the one guard went down and his friend shouted in alarm. Para heard the telling thump of two other pairs of feet on the stone flooring.

She hated being right at times.

"What the hell is that arcanist thinking having that blasted thief put traps out here? He said they were just in the first hallway, didn't he? Damn it! Where is that cleric! Blast... it's too late." The soldier uttered a string of oaths before Para made out the scuffing sound of them lifting the body and taking it away.

"I'm telling you," a soldier said, "we need to get out of this damned place. That's the fourth soldier we've lost, and at least he had a fast death. What happened to Connelly? No one knows, and that has every man spooked."

There sounded a grunt of agreement.

"Come on. Let's keep going. Anywhere is better than that place, I'm telling you."

Unfortunately, that choice had them turning the corner into Para and Mun, swords drawn and ready. The two didn't know what happened, it went down so fast. There was a scuffle and a collection of muttered curses, but then the soldiers were disarmed and tied up, stuffed in the previously discovered alcove to keep them from alerting the others. Para snickered at the dazed expressions in their blank stares as the hidden wall grumbled closed. That was always the most fun when taking people unawares: Their look of complete and utter confusion.

"I don't know when I've had this much fun," she said to Mun.

"The fun will likely cease once we meet up with the man they discussed, to say nothing of the cleric and thief they mentioned."

Para frowned at the warrior. "You do that on purpose."

"I'm simply stating the facts as I see them."

"Aye, but you don't allow me any time to enjoy the moment before doing it," she complained. "It's hardly fair, and I think you enjoy it."

Mun stared at her, nonplussed, and then looked away after a slight sigh.

"Do you need me to check for traps anymore?" Henry asked. "They said there weren't any."

"I guess it's a bit much, eh? Keep your eyes open, but no. You can be off the hook for that."

"Good. I like looking around down here. There is a lot of old stuff."

"Old stuff?" Para repeated, her eyebrow arching as she rested fists on hips. She shifted her gaze to their surroundings. She saw old stone and dust, cobwebs, and bones in certain corners of the corridor, but no 'old stuff' that would incur interest from a sylvan. "Henry, what are you talking about when you say 'old stuff'?"

Henry pointed to the framing of the corridor, which to Para only seemed to be molding and rotting girders of wood. "There's old gold gilding under all that ichor."

Both her eyebrows shot upward and she snatched an arrow from the quiver on her back, using the fletching to wipe the slimy blackness away. As the sylvan had reported, the gleam of gold, and that etched with runes, winked at her. "Well I'll be a— I'm sorry I doubted you, Henry." She focused on Derek, who regarded the gold with wide-eyed astonishment. "Milord Priest, what do you know about this basement? Was it built with the palace?"

"I always assumed such to be the case," he said, shaking his head in wonder. "I suppose I'm wrong in that assumption. It seems this basement is of a different genre than the palace."

"That's what I had in my mind as well. Interesting, that."

"Perhaps the basement maze had been here long before the palace," Mun offered, "the remnants of an old castle built upon by the Kensingtons when they first settled this area?"

Para absently nodded as she continued to stare up at the gold, her hands on her hips and her eyes narrowed in contemplation. "Now wouldn't that be an interesting bit of history?"

"Par."

"Aye, Milord Meek, I know we haven't the time to figure at the moment," she acknowledged with a slight nod. "Once we figure everything else, then maybe we'll take a gander at the history books in the libraries upstairs and see what we can see."

Henry raised his hand. "I'll go!"

"Milord Sidgwick," Para said, chuckling, "we need you down here with us as we continue around this maze. Don't you want to be part of this adventure? You seem to be on the handy side when we have you around."

"But I want to read about this basement! What if it was an arcanist's place that was blown up centuries before the Kensingtons built on it? What if it was an elfin fortress built millennia ago? What if—"

"What if it was just an old castle built by a man that liked gold?" she countered.

Henry frowned at her. "You're no fun."

"Aye, that I'm not when one of my group wants to traipse upstairs and possibly get himself killed."

The sylvan laughed. "You're funny."

"You might be an elf, Milord Sidgwick, but you're not immortal. And if you happen to run into the experimenting arcanist? What then?"

"Psh. Arcanist, shmarcanist. I'm not afraid of him."

"And why's that, pray?" Derek questioned with interest.

Henry's bright eyes darted away. "I'm just not."

"Henry Sidgwick," Para protested, grabbing his arm, "you're hiding something from us, your friends!"

"It's more fun that way!"

He pulled his arm free and scurried down the hallway the soldiers had taken with their fallen comrade. Mun and the others took off after him with shouts of "Come back! Henry!" flowered by a few curses and oaths. Henry turned a corner and there sounded a crash and a collection of angry shouts of "Intruder! Hold him!" moments before Para rounded the same with sword drawn. She smashed the first soldier in the face with her pommel.

Chaos ensued soon thereafter.

A pain-filled shout rent the air near Henry's location and one of the soldiers loosed his hold, clawing at his face as the smell of singed hair and skin filled the corridor. Para didn't have time enough to do much more than register the sound and the smell as she busied herself with parrying, dodging, and lunging at the three soldiers that surrounded her.

She bumped into a towering frame behind her and turned, sword at the ready. She pulled up short when she saw Mun, his back to her, holding his own against three others. Derek had pulled Henry free from the melee, drawing him back a safe distance from the scuffling before taking up his mace and readying himself for action. The priest didn't charge into the fore. He waited for them to come to him—none of which were free enough from their dealings with Para and Mun to do such a thing.

The close quarters made it difficult for any and all of them to move. In fact, it caused one of the soldiers to gouge out the eye of his comrade directly behind him, leaving Para more room to manipulate the swing of her sword. Distracted by the wound to his comrade, the soldier didn't see her lunge until it was too late to do much more than stare down at her in shock, blood trickling out of the side of his mouth as he slipped off her blade and crumpled to the floor.

That brought the fracas down to one on her side. Unfortunately, he chose to turn and run, giving Para no other course than to run after him to keep him from spreading the news of the group's arrival. She vaguely heard the sound of feet running after her, Derek's voice shouting back to Mun that he would follow after her to ensure her health.

The soldier had a quick step, which was the only reason Para couldn't palm and chuck a dagger at the culprit. She had to put all her effort into catching up to him. There simply wasn't enough time to get a good shot—and then he rounded a corner and shouted "Intruders! To arms, to arms!"

Para's temper red-lined, and while she wanted nothing more than to collide into the group of soldiers that were around the corner, reason won her over. Instead, she skidded to a stop and ran back the way she had come, grabbing Derek by the arm and dragging him along behind her for a few feet until he was able to catch his footing.

"Look alive, Munwar!" she yelled ahead. "We have a party coming!"

"Come ahead!" was Mun's return, causing a vague thought of curiosity just before she rounded the corner and dashed past him, Derek on her heels. "Now, Master Sidgwick!" the warrior ordered.

Para drew up and turned, watching in wide-eyed amazement as a massive ball of fire surged forth from Henry's hands down the corridor. One – two – three – four – five seconds and then the walls of the corridor shook with an explosion and a gust of hot air set her onto her haunches, the smoke and stench from singed clothes, hair and flesh springing tears to her eyes and setting them all to coughing.

"What was that?" she coughed, wiping the tears from her eyes and cheeks. She accepted Derek's help to her feet.

Henry beamed with pride, his arms crossed as Mun rested a hand on the sylvan's shoulder. "Master Sidgwick is an arcanist."

Fourteen

"A *what?*" Para stared at the sylvan, wide eyed. "Why didn't you say something?"

"It's more fun this way."

"For the love of— Make certain it isn't 'more fun' for you to watch us drop one by one, Milord Sylvan. Or else I'll haunt you the rest of your days!"

Of course Henry thought that uproariously funny. He laughed so hard after they started down the corridor that they had to push him along every other step or so. If it had been up to Para, she would have chucked him down the nearest stair.

She took hold of Henry's shirt collar to give him a slight shake. He continued to grin up at her. "Stop that sniggering, Milord Sylvan, and tell me where we've got ourselves to." Para focused on Derek and Mun. "Does anyone have any inkling where we might be under the palace? I want to get in the direction of the fountain, and at the moment we could be in the fifth ring of the god of Death's realm for as much as I know."

"I believe we are south of the fountain," Mun observed, "south and several steps west."

"Good enough. Let's try and keep stepping that direction. I want to see what there is beneath that place." The fact that Miss Pomeroy began and ended there – to say nothing of the reddening water – was a point of interest she was determined to look into.

"Para," Derek asked, falling into step beside her, "do you think we will find her... find her body?"

She tried to ignore the tautness of his lips as he regarded her. "I'm not saying we could or couldn't, Milord Priest. That place keeps giving me a tingle in the back of my head I would like to scratch."

"She has been gone for almost seven months," Derek reminded. "Certainly she must be...."

A rotting corpse? But Para chose not to finish the priest's statement. "There are a lot of different things that could be going on with her. And any of that could be because of the mysterious experimenting arcanist." *And didn't a soldier say something about a cleric?* "Arcanists always put a different spin on things, so the best thing would be to stay away from thinking anything. Just keep your eyes and mind open to what could be. Not easy, I know, but it's the only bit of advice I can give at the moment."

Derek nodded with an almost absent-minded expression as he focused ahead, his hands clenched white-fisted on the mace in his hands.

Para stopped, halting Derek with a hand on his arm. "Derek, if she's gone beyond, the best thing you can do is to focus on what you can change. Now, I don't know what that entails for a priest: Resurrecting one that's been beyond the beyond for as long, or as short, as she has? But if that's what you need, then that's what I can give you."

The priest offered a very slight smile. "Thank you. That helps."

She gave a brusque nod and continued on, moving to the head of the group and leaving Mun to the tail-end, Henry and Derek in the middle. She did her best to not think further about the history of the place, or its lack, and kept her eyes and attention focused ahead.

But the fact the basement had very few rooms along the way bothered her. They had only found two so far, and those for soldier bunks. So, it seemed the basement was more a labyrinth or dungeon, considering the corridors. With labyrinths came arcanists, vampires, lich kings, or some type of evil Minotaur creature. Those were never a good time, no matter how good the resident warrior.

The creaking of an opening door brought Para up short. She lifted a hand to motion for quiet as she continued to focus on the whereabouts of the sound. Another creak and she pointed down the corridor and to the left. On the third and fourth creaks Para began to notice a rhythm, as if it were made by a door blown by a breeze. *A breeze in a labyrinth?* That could mean a draft from an outside source, which could mean that they approached an exit.

She couldn't decide if she liked the notion or not.

Once the group reached the end of the corridor, Para hemmed and hawed about how to proceed. She wasn't so set on ducking her head around a blind corner at this particular moment, and she didn't think that sending Henry along his way would be much different—no matter how stealthy the sylvan could travel.

"I suppose it's a foolish question, but would anyone happen to have a mirror?" she whispered. She hadn't thought to bring one, so she doubted anyone else in the party had.

They all set to work searching their pouches and pockets, most all of them just for show... with the exception of Derek who brought one out of his pouch. Para raised an eyebrow, especially when she saw that it was a lady's hand-held style that fit in the palm of her hand with ease.

The engraved initials of A.E.M.P. answered any questions.

She nodded her thanks and set to the use of it, sticking it out just far enough to take a look at what was further down. *Interesting that he'd have her mirror, don't you think, Par?*

She focused the mirror on the door. "Ah. It's off one hinge, so it's swinging a bit. There is a light beyond, so we'd best trip along on the careful side of things."

Handing the mirror back, she noticed the priest's reddening ears as he accepted it and hurried to tuck it away. *She was in love with him,* she reminded, *so maybe she gave it over?* Stranger things than that had been done by women in love.

She motioned down toward the opened door. "I'm going to have a look. All you wait here. Come running if I give a holler, would you?"

"Par, do you think that wise?" Mun asked in a low voice. His brow furrowed. "We don't know what could be roaming still in these halls."

"I know that, which makes me want to take a peek around the door there. I can come and report to you what's on the other side, so we can plan."

It was plain that Mun didn't like the idea of her being separated from the rest. Para wasn't too thrilled with the idea either, but she wanted to know what waited on the other side of the door before leading their half experienced and half inexperienced group over the threshold, although Henry was turning out to be on the experienced side of things.

"Mun, I'll be fine. Just keep your ears open for some quick steps on my part, keep Henry ready with another one of those balls of fire, and keep Derek ready with a nice healing spell. Nice and simple, right?" She sent them a wink and then headed down the corridor. She didn't get two steps before Mun hissed and recalled her attention.

Stepping forward, he offered her his lucky token. "Take this."

"Now this is getting ridiculous. I'm just going to scout ahead," she protested as she eyed the token.

"I know, but take it just the same." He pressed the token into her palm and then turned back for the group.

She stared down at it for a time or three before tossing it up into the air and catching it behind her back, giving it a collection of flips between her fingers and then tucking it into her pouch. Then she patted it and turned again to make her way down the corridor, wishing that having the little token didn't make her feel better.

Before she rounded the corner she crouched, listening to the surrounding sounds while feeling the stone flooring for any hint of heavy steps. The air was still, giving no hint of anything beyond the doors, and the silence didn't seem out of the ordinary for a stone labyrinth. The only thing that bothered her was the rhythmic squeak of the lopsided door.

Well, Par, what do you think? She didn't want to open the door, is what she thought. But there was no way to know what hung on the other side without doing something, and in order to do that she had to venture around the corner— Para's gaze darted to her right and down into the grinning face of Henry Sidgwick.

She frowned at him, not wanting to risk a hiss of disapproval nor a whispered order to get back with the others. It wouldn't have done much good anyway because the others were directly behind the sylvan, Mun at the very end.

Henry skirted around Para, dodging her attempt to grab him by the scruff or the belt. He crept to the area behind the door and peeked through the crack between door and stone opening. The amount of time he invested in the spying gave Para time to cool her temper and restrain the urge to bash the men's heads together.

The sylvan returned on quick and silent steps, shaking his head. Why he didn't feel it safe enough to speak had Para's curiosity piqued and the hairs on the nape of her neck standing on end. *The little shrub likely doesn't want to go first.* She didn't blame him one bit, to be honest. She didn't feel like going first either.

She pressed her lips together and then turned the corner, doing her best to tread as silent as possible before risking a peek beyond the door. The room was brightly lit, but all she saw were tables, beakers, jars, cages... and a table on the far side on which lay the silhouette of a form. It was enough out of the angle of her glance that she couldn't tell what it could be.

Para motioned to the others. They crept around and positioned themselves just behind her, flat against the wall. She motioned that she planned to enter the room and pointedly ignored Mun's disapproving frown. Someone had to do it, and she couldn't in all conscience have it be the little shrub.

Gauging the amount of space the door allowed, she eased herself through while taking careful stock of her surroundings. The room was twice as large as the experiment room on the second floor and had many of the same arrangements of paraphernalia, plus a few more questionable items; the most noticeable of those being a collection of mangled weaponry.

Some had broken blades, others exploded pommels, and one axe had been submerged into the table blade deep. It made Para wonder what the arcanist was attempting to discover. *Something for the General?* she mused. *Something for Lord Kensington senior? Do they not even know the arcanist is down here?*

Anything was possible.

The table and the form upon it drew Para's attention, the form hidden by a sheet. A sudden shiver up and down her spine made her decide against venturing over. Instead, she turned to the duty of widening the opening of the door without causing a din.

While the act of opening the door wide enough for Mun to slip through did elicit an elongated squeak, it didn't attract any undue attention. In fact, the silence of the room began to pick and chew at Para's calm, causing her to send darting glances over her shoulder to different portions of the room—all away from the table with the sheet-covered form.

"What is this place?" Derek asked in as low a whisper as he could manage.

Henry, who grimaced while pinching his nose, volunteered the correct answer. "It's an arcanist's room. He's practicing bad spellings here."

Bad spellings? With the way Para's shivers continued, she wouldn't be a bit surprised. It didn't help that the room smelled about as horrid as a swamp. Para fingered a couple of vials on a table, one labeled '*dire*' and the other '*winter*.' They were filled with a reddish liquid that, again, sent the shivers up and down her spine and made the hairs on the back of her neck dance around. She wiped her fingers on her breeches and stepped away from the table.

"Henry, what can you tell us about some of these things?" she asked in a low voice. "Besides the whole 'bad spellings' theory. Something else?" Something that would explain why an arcanist would be in a labyrinth beneath the Kensington palace would have been very welcome at that point in time. Maybe it was his labyrinth in the first place? Maybe he was about a million years old— *Par! Get a hold of yourself!*

She palmed a dagger and scratched a long scar into the table top.

Looking up, she noticed that Henry hadn't heard a bit of her question. Instead, he focused on the table beside her and the two beakers of reddish liquid. The way his eyes narrowed made the little shrub actually appear a bit on the dangerous side and, quite frankly, it gave her pause. In fact, the entire palace and its basement had been 'giving her pause' off and on for the entire week. She would be glad to be rid of the mystery so that she could venture off somewhere else. *Carmaline is supposed to be nice this year.*

Or maybe get off the nation altogether.

Para snapped her fingers in front of Henry's face, jolting back his attention and causing the sylvan's ears to pink. It was the first time she had ever seen an elf embarrassed. "Henry, what has you grabbed?" Picking up a vial, she waved it in front of his attention like a pendulum; his gaze locked and followed the action.

After several drawn moments of continued silence – the heady quiet even drawing Derek and Mun's attention – Para hid the vial behind her back and leaned down into the sylvan's personal space. He startled and stepped back.

"Something you might want to tell us, Milord Sidgwick?"

"N-No."

"Aye, is that right?" She brought the vial around again and noticed his immediate draw, although this time he put up a bit of resistance to the desire to look. "Nothing of interest about this little bottle here?" She reached behind her for the other vial without turning and showed it as well. "Or this one? Something of interest to us maybe? Hm?"

With admirable fortitude, Henry drug his gaze from the two vials, his face going quite pale, and focused on Para. "Those are very bad," he whispered.

Para straightened, her scrutiny shifting to the vials in her hand. "Bad? They're just a bit of poison of some kind. For wolves? Isn't that what 'dire' and 'winter' are? Kinds of wolves?"

Stepping to Para's side, Mun extended a hand. "May I see?" He accepted one of the vials from Para and performed an intense examination of the vials. "Interesting."

"What is? It's just a vial."

"That's what is so interesting. Why would such a thing bother Milord Sidgwick?" He offered it toward the sylvan, shocked when the sylvan twitched and stepped back. Henry even tucked his hands close to his chest. "Milord?"

"It's blood," he squeaked out.

"What?" Para's hold on the vial almost gave way. "Blood? Blood of what?"

"W-wolves."

Letting loose an assortment of expletives expressing her irritation, she deposited the vial back onto the table and wiped her hand onto her breeches. "Can we say how much I'm beginning to hate this place?" she muttered. She wiped at her eyes. The reek of the place was burning her nose and making her eyes water. "What in the name of all that's— what does he need with wolf blood? Do I even want to know?"

Henry opened his mouth to answer, but Para cut him off with a raised hand. "No. I don't. Everything about this place stinks to the five hells, and I'm just about done. Let's get this mystery solved and get out. The minute I stepped into this room, all the spirit of adventure oozed out of me."

Mun grumbled in agreement as he stepped from the vials toward the sheet-covered table. Para noticed his reach for the sheet too late, for though she hissed "Mun, no!" it wasn't in time. He pulled back the sheet to reveal a heinously disfigured woman with dark tresses.

Para and Mun both retched.

Derek sounded a heart-rending cry from the back of the room and stumbled toward the table. Gripping the table edge, he stared down into the mutilated face. "Alicia… no…."

Keeping her gaze carefully away, Para pulled the sheet up to cover the face. "You sure of that, Milord Priest?" she gasped.

The priest's shoulders sagged and he lowered his head.

"If you're sure," she pressed, "then you can do what you need to have some peace; be that giving last rights or saying the prayer that will have her sitting up. Once that's done, we'll step on out of here and put the question to your brother about the goings on in this infernal place."

His only answer was a slight shake of his head.

Nona King | 173

"All right. We'll keep on and see what else there is to this nightmare."

Para didn't really have a resounding desire to know at the moment, and she greatly respected the priest's restraint in continuing with the search. She didn't know how easy it was for a priest to go about asking for a resurrection here and a resurrection there. What if he could only ask once? If he asked got it, and this poor girl was only some missing lady from a different city altogether?

Not a good time.

She patted his back before stepping from the table to continue her examination of the chamber. Mun followed behind, using his sleeve to wipe any remaining foulness from his face. Henry continued to stare at the vials of blood, which made Para grimace and rub her hands on her breeches.

"Henry," she hissed, finally gathering his attention. "Will you stop staring at those foul things? If it bothers you so much, we'll chuck them out the window." She motioned toward them. "What would he use that nastiness for anyway?"

The sylvan's gaze searched the room and came to rest on the collection of weaponry. He lifted a sword with an exploded pommel. "This."

"What? He uses it to destroy weapons?"

Henry laughed, and the sound helped Para relax a little. "You're funny."

"Stop saying that and tell me."

"He uses the blood, and many other potions and tinctures, to create ensorcelled weaponry."

"Ensorcelled— you mean, spell infused?" Henry nodded, and Para lowered her scrutiny to the long sword at her waist. "How do you know if a sword has that done?"

"You pay an arcanist to do a reading."

She tapped a rhythm on the scabbard belt and then sloughed

it off, deciding to stop by the secret armory to do an exchange of this sword for her old one. If there was a chance that the arcanist had done anything out of the ordinary to it, she wanted no part of the thing.

"Bah," she grumbled, turning for the only other door that led out of the chamber. "I've had about enough of this room. Let's see what we can see through here. I still have yet to find the underside of the fountain and would like to do that before I hear the tattle of Miss Pomeroy's song start up."

Para caught Mun's glance toward the sheet-covered form and the priest that continued to stand over it with lowered head and clasped hands. As before, there shone a pale light around him as he prayed whatever his heart led.

The intensity with which he sought solace for the unknown woman impressed Para the most. What was his motivation other than the thought it could be the woman whom everyone suspected him of killing? Was the best way to alleviate suspicion to resurrect his only witness?

His determination to seek out Alicia's body and resurrect her gave one pause to think of him as the murderer. At least, it gave more credence to the thought of his innocence.

"Milord Priest?" she ventured in a quiet tone of urgency.

The priest released a slow and deep breath, the shining ebbing into nothing as he lowered his hands and then lifted his head. He offered Para a forced smile that only faintly lifted the corners of his mouth. If anything it made the pain in his features all the more prominent.

"Keep your hopes, Milord," she urged in a low tone. *'Look to the sunrise and there will be hope,'* she wanted to tell him. Unfortunately, she wasn't so sure he could handle the quote from the girl. "For the sake of Miss Alicia, keep your hopes." It would have to be good enough.

He nodded, the area around his lips whiting—

Nona King | 175

The door opened of its own volition, drawing four sets of startled gazes to the two men standing just as startled in the now open doorway.

Fifteen

The shocked silence vanished with the clang and hiss of drawn swords.

"I believe you were told another trespass would have definite consequences, Ranger," the General rumbled in his harsh bass voice.

Derek Kensington stepped forward. "Brother, stop this! I care little about who is responsible, or the reasons why Miss Pomeroy vanished. I only want to give her soul peace!"

Cyruss' granite features hardened as he sheathed his sword. He continued to glare at his younger sibling. "You are a fool, Derek, allowing your sensibilities to cower within you. Take control of your life! Don't hide behind weakness, catering to the widowed and orphaned. This will not make you a better man."

To Para it seemed the brothers didn't care much one for the other. *Interesting that,* she mused as she sheathed her own sword. Mun followed her lead, though his countenance clearly read of his wariness.

"And you?" Derek retorted, "Are you the better man, Cyruss? You who command so many; you who slaughter the innocent to feed your lust for power; is that 'a man'?"

"Bah! What do you know of what life requires to live? You, tucked away in that church of brick and glass, helping those who are too lazy to help themselves. I fight for your protection, Brother, for the coin that jingles in your coffers, for the tallow candles that light your devoted studies."

"Where was Alicia's protection?"

The quiet question caused a twitch to the General's jaw muscle as a vein bulged at his temple. Para watched the reaction with interest and sent Mun a sidelong glance. The warrior watched the two brothers with keen intensity. The arcanist behind the General also seemed to wait with baited breath for the outcome of this stand-off.

"Did you so hate what she stood for, Brother, that her innocence meant nothing? Was her station such a—"

"Be silent, you fool!" The General's harsh command caused Mun and Para both to adjust their stance and shift their hands to their weaponry. "You make me ill, speaking of hate and innocence. What do you know of passions and pleasantries such as these?"

"This is ridiculous," Para mumbled. She stepped forward, reaching out an arm to come between the brothers and press Derek back a step. She met and held the General's hard glare. "General, I have one question for you, and how you choose to answer it will determine how you leave this room."

Cyruss' lips twisted in a wry smile. "And what, pray, is the question, Ranger?"

"What did you do with the body of Miss Alicia Pomeroy after you pushed her off the balcony?" Para noticed a twitch from the arcanist standing behind the General. He glanced toward the sheet-covered form.

The General scoffed. "Certainly you don't believe I am a fool, Ranger? I have nothing more to say on the matter of Miss Pomeroy's untimely disappearance."

She hadn't really expected any other answer. "Fool? No, likely not. But I bet your arcanist friend there will have something to say on the matter." The horror in the arcanist's gaze was hard to miss as he shrank back.

"I will have him contact you tomorrow. At present, you are trespassers and I shall escort you off the premises forthwith."

"I don't think so, General. We've a mystery to solve and, 'at present,' you're in the way. One side or the other; makes no difference as long as you move." The expression of incredulity on the General's face was priceless, causing Para a glowing feeling of amusement.

"Ranger," the General spoke in a low voice, "you are trying my patience."

"Is that it then? You've nothing to say and so 'off you go?' Not a bit of help one way or the other, are you?" The elder Kensington traipsed all over her last nerve.

"Step aside before I forcibly move you."

"Aye, you're good at that aren't you, General? Did Miss Pomeroy not step aside for you?"

"Bah! I've little time for this, Ranger. Stand aside or the consequences be damned," he warned, making good on the threat as he drew his sword. Para and Mun unsheathed theirs in the same moment, the light from the glowing runes of Mun's blade casting an eerie glow of shadow in the chamber.

Derek once again intervened, his expression alight with a dangerous calm that reminded Para of the elder Kensington. Not only that, a resonating light surrounded the priest and gave her a case of the shivers.

"What have you done, Brother? Have you sold your soul, then, to this black wizard so that you may have more power? Was that the price Alicia paid? Her life for the power of your armies?" Derek pointed a finger at the arcanist who cowered behind the General's seething form. "You will find little mercy from me, Wizard. Your life is forfeit to my god's judgment."

As Derek took a threatening step forward, the arcanist

wailed in alarm and pushed the General forward, making good his escape in the confusion thereafter. The General, unprepared for the sudden offense against his balance, stumbled forward and onto Para's blade, staring down at her in gaping astonishment as she blinked up into his widened eyes. His jaw worked several times before he slumped, sliding off the blade into a heap at her feet.

"What the—"

"Par! The priest!" Mun shouted, darting after Derek Kensington who took off after the retreating arcanist.

Para's astonishment crumbled and she sprinted after Mun. At the other end of the short corridor Derek beat his shoulder against a decrepit but firmly closed door.

"Stand clear!" Mun bellowed. He lowered his head and shoulder to sprint the final steps. Para had never seen him travel at a faster pace or thunder quite so loudly.

The wood splintered but remained intact enough to require a joint effort. The second collision collapsed the door and sent Derek stumbling into the room beyond with only partial control of his footing. The arcanist spun and shrunk back against the far wall of the chamber. A marble table stood between them and upon that lie another sheet-enshrouded figure.

Derek's gaze didn't waver from the darting eyes of the arcanist. "Say penance for your soul, Wizard, for today you meet the judgment you deserve."

Considering the experimentation equipment of the other room, to say nothing of the ensorcelled armor and weaponry, Para felt fairly certain the arcanist was of a greater level than Derek could handle.

"Derek, I wouldn't be too hasty—"

He spun, his brown eyes determined as they held her gaze. "You need not be a part of this, Milady."

Frowning, Para scoffed. "I haven't yet stepped away from—

"

"Para!" Henry called. The sylvan's shout was followed immediately by a growl, and that by a squeal that made Para and Mun sprint from the room. The walls shook with a blood curdling roar from some type of animal, and the next instant a little shrub of a sylvan tore down the corridor toward them, a werewolf at his heels wearing the remnants of a soldier's uniform.

"What in Nefa's—" She lowered her gaze to the sword in her hands, the wolf blood on the table, the various exploded weapons in this chamber— Para dropped the sword in horror.

The werewolf drew up, its mouth slathered with drool and flecks of foam as its wild gaze narrowed in regard of the three.

Para sent a sidelong glance to the broad sword at Mun's belt. "Mun, I think the sword—"

The beast lunged.

Mun deflected the brunt of the attack, grunting as the power of the thing pushed him into Para. She heard the creak of leather as his grip tightened on his father's claymore and he swung at the beast. "We have no silver!"

Pushing the sylvan back toward the other door, she gripped his arm. "It's up to you, Henry! Mun can hold the thing off, but only you and your spells can kill him."

Wide eyed and pale, Henry nodded.

"Good lad." Palming two daggers, she focused on the beast as she stepped to the wall and crouched into the shadows. She had to be careful to concentrate solely on fading into the darkness and walking in silence. If she lost focus at all any advantage she had against the creature would be lost, her life along with it.

Para crept around the grappling pair of warrior and werewolf, only vaguely aware of Henry beginning his casting.

Mun deflected a slash and bite, incurring the creature's wrathful snarl. Para leapt from the shadows, her dagger submerging hilt-deep into the flesh near his spine. Howling in agony, the creature arched its back, opening itself to the lunge and thrust from Mun's claymore.

Blood pooled at the creature's feet as it snapped for Mun with its powerful jaws, but the sudden motion caused a lurch as it slipped in its own ichor.

Throwing herself back from an attempted bite, Para stumbled and fell just as a cascade of bright lights shot from the roof of the corridor. The lights pummeled the werewolf, raining down upon his head and shoulders and pressing him against the floor.

Para bolted upright, freeing her bow in the same motion and sending an arrow into the back of the werewolf's head. It snarled biting at Mun as it attempted to stagger to its feet. Mun slashed at its shoulder and shouted a warning to Henry who scurried past him to the werewolf, not stopping until he had grabbed the creature's head. Flames flared from the sylvan's hands and consumed the entire creature.

It howled and roared, snarling at Henry with its last ounce of strength. Then it went still, the blackened form occasionally twitching as Henry stepped back. The three stared down at the thing, their heavy breathing the only sound in the corridor—there sounded a crash behind them and all three turned as one.

"Derek!" Para shouted as she sprinted forward. *How could you forget about the priest?* She scolded.

They dove into the chamber, staring in surprise at Derek Kensington as he stood over the unconscious form of the arcanist. They both looked disheveled, their robes and tunics torn and singed. There were also tell-tale smudges and bruising to their faces that confessed a fist fight and not just a case of the divine versus the arcane.

Derek turned at their entrance, wiping the blood from the side of his mouth as he offered them a wince and a smile. The smile vanished, however, when shrouded form on the table drew his gaze. He staggered forward, staring down at the white sheet for several moments before pulling it back and revealing the lovely yet ashen face of Alicia Pomeroy.

Sixteen

Para nervously tapped her fingers against the thighs of her breeches, her gaze drawn to the door into the corridor. "Is it about time Miss Pomeroy makes a show upstairs? Or is it later than that?" *How long did it take for that soldier to turn?* Of course, there was no way for her to know if it was the soldier she killed the day before. "Henry, can you go check if the General's body is still in the chamber?"

Mun rested a hand on Henry's shoulder. "I will go, Master Sidgwick."

"Mun, Henry is the only one—"

"Then I will go with him," Mun said, his jaw set.

"Aye, aye." Para ran a hand through her short-cut red hair. "I have the jitters of a sudden." She sent Derek a sidelong glance as he continued to stare into the pale beauty of Miss Pomeroy. "Go on Mun, Milord Henry. The priest and I will figure what to do next about Miss Pomeroy. You see about the General."

"If the body is gone…." Mun ventured.

"Aye. We'll have a real problem on our hands." She looked to the arcanist, still unconscious amongst the debris on the floor of the chamber. *I guess we'll have to keep a hold of him for a while.* The last thing they needed were more lycanthropes – werewolves – running around. If the General became one because of her sword, he would need to be contained so that he couldn't have the chance to infect others.

Mun regarded Para in thoughtful seriousness before urging Henry out of the chamber. She shifted her focus to the priest. His hold tightened on both the table and the holy symbol hanging from the cord around his waist.

"So what's to do next, Milord Priest? We've got a body. We've got a soul. How do we get them together again?" She felt as if she asked the man to tell her a nursery rhyme about a broken egg.

"There needs to be an exorcism," he said in a quiet tone.

"Lord Pomeroy didn't seem to want one of those."

Derek heaved a sigh as he drug his gaze to meet Para's. "Lord Pomeroy is a superstitious gentleman. He believes that an exorcism will cast his daughter's soul forever into an abyss, alone. He doesn't understand that Miss Pomeroy, here, and her tortured soul that reappears each night…. They are separated, joined apart. An exorcism would separate them both from their anchors, freeing them and allowing them to be joined together again, in wholeness."

"So, you can only resurrect her if you exorcise her first?"

The priest nodded. "To do that, I need to find her ghost."

"What?" Para asked sharply. "Don't you remember what happened last time we had a run in with the late Miss Pomeroy's ghost? She didn't take kindly to your face."

Again, Derek nodded, but this time he had knelt to begin drawing a circle on the ground.

Para's eyebrow twitched upward. "What are you doing?"

"Preparing. This will hold the ghost, giving me time to finish the ritual."

"A circle?"

"Yes. A circle and within it something of hers that keeps her drawn to this place." He placed the mirror within the circle, as well as a bit of pink ribbon that he pulled from the pouches at his belt. "She will remember," he said, almost to himself.

Para stepped back from the table, making herself scarce near the door into the corridor. She propped the door open enough for a hasty getaway, with the priest of course, or to see how Mun and Henry faired in their search for the General's body – if it wasn't where it was supposed to be.

She wasn't certain what an exorcism entailed in action or in reaction from the body and soul. Whether it would take a minute or a day she didn't know, but she had been on enough adventures to know things seldom ever worked out the way one first thought they should, or would. So, she set herself ready for the worst so she would be pleasantly surprised if things went faster.

They never did, but one could always look on the bright side of things.

Mun and Henry returned from the far chamber with a serious expression that bordered on morose. Para stepped into the corridor to meet them, closing the door as much as she could to muffle the sounds of their quiet discourse.

"Please tell me it was there," she said.

"It was."

Para very nearly had to sit down with the relief that wobbled her knees. "I need you and Henry to take that body out and burn it; do it in the chamber itself if you feel you've room and won't set us all ablaze. Henry, you're going to need to set it afire like you did the werewolf. Aye?"

Henry nodded.

Mun gestured to the mostly closed door. "How does Milord Priest fare?"

"He's getting ready to do an exorcism. I'm going to need to hang back here and keep our lord priest alive, if Miss Pomeroy gets another fancy to take his head for herself." She sent Mun a sidelong scrutiny as he regarded the closed door. "How long does one of those take?"

Mun tugged on his chin. "Depending on the priest, it could be an hour or nearly half a day."

Para slapped her forehead. "Aye, just the right of it, eh? And then he can go abouts doing the resurrection of the girl?"

"I don't know. A resurrection is a special skill, just as is an exorcism. Milord Kensington will need to rest in order to prepare."

She hissed her disapproval yet again. The town of Pomeroy had long since worn out its welcome. The sooner she could vanish onto its horizon the better it would be for her. "So we're likely stranded for another day?"

"At the very least."

"You're just filled with good tidings, aren't you?"

Mun looked away.

"Aye. That you are. Well, let's get ourselves to our different tasks and see what we can do about a 'The End' on this crazy bit of adventuring."

"What about the arcanist?" Henry piped up.

"What can we do to the bloke that will keep him out of mischief?"

"A good silence spell should do the trick," Henry said with a mischievous twinkle in his eyes.

"Good lad. That might be just the thing to annoy an arcanist, eh?"

Henry nodded.

I hope to high heaven this adventure is near done, she mused. She would easily sleep a week, even if she had to sell Mun's star sapphire to pay for the room.

Henry entered the chamber and set to his task. Not only did he cast silence on the arcanist, he also used leather thongs to tie the man's hands and feet to keep him from scurrying around.

Then he gave his work an approving nod and hurried out of the room just as silent as he had entered.

"All right, you two, set to work with that pyre business. Meet back here once every last bit of him has smoldered away. If anyone asks… well…." She threw up her hands. "Make something up."

Mun smirked as he nodded, giving Henry's shoulder a nudge toward the corridor and the chamber beyond. "We will need to take the sheet from Miss Marina," he told the sylvan.

Henry whined his displeasure, causing a chuckle from Para before she entered the priest's chamber. He stood over Miss Pomeroy's still and pale body in reserved silence, his hand clasping the holy symbol.

"Are you up for this, Milord Priest? Mun was saying it could take quite a bit of time."

Derek inclined his head. "He is correct, and I cannot pray for resurrection the same day as an exorcism."

"Aye. He said something similar." She came to stand on the other side of the table, staring down at Alicia Pomeroy's pale face. "It looks like she's sleeping," she mused. The girl had a lovely countenance – innocence personified, if Para had to say something to give it a name – but she also looked to be having a bad dream. "Does she know?"

"This is just a body," Derek said in a quiet tone. "A shell. It knows nothing. Feels less."

She absently nodded, a hand rubbing at the back of her neck and the raised hairs there.

The waiting for the ghost's arrival was some of the worst waiting Para ever had to do. When the ear piercing scream was heard, then the splash, both her and Derek must have gone as white as the ghost they wait for. Then there she stood in front of them, her expression pained and yet confused.

When her gaze focused on Derek, rage marred her affect into an unrecognizable ugliness. She lunged for the priest. This time, however, he didn't shrink back, standing as he was on the other side of the circle. Para, on the other hand, dodged around the table to intercept the raging ghost. She halted only when Derek shouted at her not to interfere—and just then Miss Pomeroy's ghost came to a rather sudden stop inside the circle.

Alicia's expression shifted from rage to confusion, her hands splayed out in front of her as if she sought comfort. The look on Derek's face spoke volumes.

"I am sorry, Alicia," he whispered, "but the pain will be short-lived. I promise." Derek knelt, clasping the holy symbol in his hands as he lowered his head and began to recite phrases in a language that Para didn't understand.

At first Alicia screeched, her hands and arms flailing as she turned her head this way and that. It very nearly chased Para from the room. But then an iridescent glow began to build around the priest and, after about twenty minutes, Alicia calmed enough to stare down at the priest's bowed head.

Para didn't recall hearing when Mun and Henry returned from their duty of burning the General's remains. Nor did she notice when Mun knelt and began whispering his own collection of prayers.

Henry watched the priest and warrior in curiosity and then surprise. That expression was followed by a smile of satisfaction. Then he sat back against the wall of the chamber nearest the door and toyed with his flute without a sound.

Para, on the other hand, couldn't pull her gaze from the priest and ghost. She didn't know how long she stood there watching the two and their reactions to the journey of exorcism.

What else could she call it but a journey?

Every so often Alicia's expression would twist in discomfort or she would sob and flinch in some type of pain. But Derek wouldn't lift his gaze, intent on his duty of completing the rites so that Alicia would be free to re-join the 'shell' that had been hers during life.

Looking again to Miss Pomeroy's body made Para wonder at how it didn't show the same effects as Miss Marina's—at least, she supposed the body to be Miss Marina. It was so amazingly preserved!

"Derek...."

The voice of Alicia drew Para's sharp attention moments before the ghostly visage vanished. The last expression on the girl's countenance had been that of complete and utter peace-an expression that gave Para the chills.

"What happened to her?"

Derek gathered the mirror and ribbon without lifting his gaze from the circle. "She has been freed from where she was trapped."

"Meaning?"

"She won't haunt these grounds any longer." Derek tried to stand, and at his stagger Para hurried to offer her support. "Thank you."

"Let's get you someplace to rest. Come along, Milord. I think there's a guest room upstairs calling your name."

Derek inclined his nod, barely able to motion toward Alicia's body on the table. "Please. Don't leave her here in the dark."

"Aye, aye. Mun, can you gather up the lass and bring her along with us? We'll come later and fetch the arcanist."

Mun straightened and nodded, taking up the form of the girl with hardly any effort.

"Henry, do you mind staying down here a bit and watching the old coot?"

Henry scoffed. "He doesn't scare me."

"Good lad." She focused again on Derek. His countenance was dangerously pale, dark circles giving his eyes a sunken appearance. "You need to sleep, Milord. Don't fret on the girl. We'll do right by her."

"You don't understand…. There is limited time for her soul to be bonded back to her body. Don't let me sleep past this point tomorrow. If you do, I won't have enough time to perform the resurrection rite."

"Aye, as you command, Milord. We'll keep things on schedule."

Derek leaned heavily on her as he accepted her help from the chamber. "Thank you, Milady."

This time Para decided to leave the title alone.

Seventeen

"I think he fell asleep before we were up the stairs." Para slumped onto the chair at the table in the guest room of the Kensington palace. Her gaze shifted to the young woman's pale beauty, and again she couldn't decide of the girl was truly dead or only sleeping.

She shrugged it off and focused on Mun. The warrior remained silent, his blank gaze on his clasped hands. "Aye," she said. "This bit of mystery has me just as cornered. But how do we get answers from charred remains?" She hissed her displeasure.

Mun blinked and lifted his head. "What more needs to be solved? General Kensington murdered her for his freedom."

"A bit of irony, that, for now he has it in spades."

The warrior's lips twisted in a wry smile.

"Irony aside…." The remainder of the sentence vanished as Para noticed Marina lingering in the hallway just outside the door. In fact, the maid peeked through the slight opening. "Marina?"

The maid flushed, if a ghost could do such a thing, and dropped a curtsy before self-consciously slipping into the room. "I didn't mean to disturb you."

Mun and Para exchanged curious glances. "No bother, girl. We're just chewing the air between us. Can we help you with something?"

The still body of Alicia Pomeroy drew Marina's focus to the canopy bed. An expression of quiet mourning fell over the maid's countenance. "She's truly gone, then…." The maid began to weep. "The beast…."

An eyebrow arched as Para regarded the girl.

"I hoped it wasn't so, but…." A fresh wave of sobs shook the girl's shoulders as she lifted her hands to cover her face.

Para didn't know a ghost could cry. "Now, now, girl." She stood and made her way to the ghost's side. "Miss Alicia's destiny waits a bit is all. Lord Derek the priest is set to resurrect her tomorrow. And who's to say he can't do the same for you?"

That drew the maid's wide-eyed gaze and she faltered back a step, terror marring her face. "…no…"

The reaction furrowed Para's brows. "You can't want to wander around this place forever, can you?"

The maid shook her head.

"Aye, then be a good girl and let us do something about that. 'The beast' has had his bit of justice, so there's no need to worry about whether or not your life will be the same as it was—it won't."

"But I've heard of the thing they do," Marina whispered, and she cast a quick glance behind her. "They could banish me to hell for what I done."

Para arched an eyebrow. "The Priest? He'd sooner banish his own self to the dark regions than an innocent. Come on now, girl. Don't be daft."

"But you don't know!" Marina stepped back, her arms rigid at her sides as tears flowed. "The Miss be pained because of me, and it fixes me right to wander—so I will stay, even if she be gone and coming around."

The words were nonsense to Para, and apparently to Mun as well who only shrugged when she sent him a questioning glance. "What nonsense are you spewing, girl? The General is the one that did the deed, and he's been seen to. From my sight you've been a good and decent maid, helping the Miss with her room and—"

"I couldn't stop him!" she shrieked, "I would have given my life for her and he took it without even a bit of mercy! The Miss be there because of me!"

With a final wail, Maid Marina turned and fled from the room. Para and Mun stared after her in stupefied amazement and finally bolted after her.

"What in Nefa's fire is she going on about?"

Mun shook his head.

The two came upon the maid in the chaotic mess that was her room. She sat upon her bed sobbing into her hands crying, "I could have stopped him; I could have saved her; why didn't I save her?" in a tone that had the hairs on Para's neck dancing along with the rhythm.

"Snap out of it, girl!" Para scolded. "You're not much bigger than a pet dog and you think—"

Resting his hand upon her shoulder, Mun interrupted her tirade. Para pressed her lips into a thin white line.

"Miss Marina," Mun spoke in a gentle tone as he knelt in front of her weeping form, "your loyalty to your mistress has been commendable, though you feel you have failed her in this one important duty. You should not squander the life waiting based on that failure. Not when so many victories lie in your wake."

"Oh Milord, how can I look upon her face knowing I did nothing?" She wept, her voice muffled by her trembling hands.

"You can look upon her face because she knows you did all that was possible for you. Now she has need of your care and your loyalty."

Marina's weeping had ebbed as the warrior spoke. Now the girl raised her glimmering eyes to his stoic gaze, somehow taking courage and comfort from what she saw there. She offered him a hesitant smile and a slight nod. "Thank you, Milord," she whispered.

Well I'll be a... Para gave a bewildered shake of her head and turned away. With the way the world was turning on its ear, warriors growing philosophical, she wouldn't be surprised if pigs flew outside.

※

The next morning the priest continued to sleep.

They moved the arcanist to a bare room on the first floor where both Mun and Henry alternated in keeping him under guard. Lord Pomeroy sent a messenger to Lord Kensington senior in Arielle requesting a discourse in person regarding the state of their families. Para hadn't wanted to tell him about the impending resurrection attempt of his daughter, so she left well enough alone when the Lord sent her a message informing her of his decision to contact the Kensington head.

She also gave the messenger a bit of something extra when he promised not to hustle to and fro.

Derek woke in the later morning asking for water and food. Para obliged, offering him a hearty stew she had brought from *The Journeyman's Palace* as well as her water skin. He ate like a man who hadn't eaten in a week and then, very few minutes later, drifted off to sleep again.

At just after noon, about the time Para began to get antsy, Derek opened his eyes. He stared at the ceiling for several quiet minutes while clasping his holy symbol to his chest. Then he sat up and swung his legs over the side of the bed, gripping the mattress as he stared down at the floorboards and his soft-soled boots.

Para began to wonder if he had second thoughts about the resurrection.

Then he took in a deep breath and pulled on his boots, determination darkening his brown eyes as he stood. He offered her a greeting nod and a slight smile. "Para, shall we go?"

One eyebrow twitched as she stood, motioning toward the door of the guest room before proceeding through it ahead of him. He followed her across the hall to Alicia's room in contemplative silence, the clink of the beads of his holy symbol hinting at his thoughtful mood. Once they entered Alicia's room he made his way to the girl's bed, Para hanging back by the door. Like the exorcism, she didn't know what went into a resurrection and she didn't want to be under foot.

Derek sat on the edge of the bed, covering Alicia's clasped hands with his and staring down into her peaceful countenance for a long and silent moment. Then he drew a small vial from a pouch at his belt and dabbed the liquid with a single finger. This finger then traced the symbol of a cross on Miss Pomeroy's forehead while he, again, whispered a collection of phrases that sounded to be a language older than old.

The door beside her opened to reveal Mun. His focus didn't stray from the priest and the girl. "Wait outside, Para. I will tend to the priest."

"So tend to the priest, but I'm staying here," she whispered. Who knew when she would have another opportunity to see a rite like this?

That drew a sidelong glance from the warrior. He made his way toward the other side of the girl's bed and knelt. It was only the second time she saw the warrior pray, and again she began to wonder if there wasn't something more than tending to the priest. She heard many a tale of warriors following clerics, usually accompanied by a transformation. She wasn't quite sure what to think about any of it, especially not with Mun kneeling right there in front of her—

The iridescent glow returned to the priest, this time brighter than ever, and with it materialized the ghostly visage of Alicia Pomeroy at the foot of the bed. Para restrained a hiss, her hand hovering over the pommel of her rapier as she watched the ghost girl for any hint of a negative action. But she only continued to gaze at the bowed head of the priest, her expression unreadable.

Then, when Para began to doubt the girl wanted to come back, she shifted her haunting attention to her own body and stepped forward. Each step had her visage fading and the color returning to her body's skin. Then the final step was taken, the ghost vanished and Alicia gasped and choked out a name, her hands flailing as if to catch at some familiar thing.

Derek caught her hand in his and pulled it close, his eyes focused on her face. "I am here, Alicia…" he said in a quiet tone.

At the sound of his voice she calmed, her eyes focusing on his for a long moment before she smiled. "I knew you wouldn't leave me in the dark," she whispered.

Para allowed a slight upward twitch of lip and then turned to leave the room.

Epilogue

"So where are we bound now, Milord Meek?"

The warrior accepted his pint of ale from the barkeep at *The Journeyman's Palace* and offered him a coin. The barkeep waved it aside and left them.

"I need to stay," he informed her.

"For what? We've done our bit of adventuring. Lord Pomeroy has settled our wage, and Miss Pomeroy and Milord Priest are friends again." Para leaned toward the warrior and elbowed him. "How long do you think before they're able to find a way to be wed?"

"Par—"

"Aye, aye. I know," she acknowledged with a frown and a slight wave. "It's a fool's business, love. I swear it off. Mark my words." She took a long draught of her ale. "So, where are we bound?"

"I need to stay," Mun said again.

"For *what?*" Para's annoyance flickered in her green eyes. "We've a hefty sum jingling in our pockets, the Lords and Ladies are happy all around, and there hasn't been sight nor sound of any more werewolves—Though, come to think of it, we still haven't popped open that secret room Master Sidgwick found. Remember the one? On the second floor; the room with all the broken beakers?"

"I remember."

Para regarded her warrior friend with a narrowed gaze. The way his scrutiny did not waver from his mug of ale had her red hair bristling. "Munwar Meek. Don't tell me you've a plot and ploy to crack open that bit of room to take all the wealth for yourself!"

Mun actually scoffed, and his hard gaze finally lifted to meet hers. "There was naught in that room but evil, and this land has plenty of such to satisfy."

Her eyebrow arched. "Satisfy? Satisfy what?"

The warrior didn't seem want to answer. "My studies."

"Studies? Of what? With who?" Her face twisted in confusion. "There's not a higher level warrior at the smithy, is there? And what would having evil abouts do with that anyway?"

"It matters little to you, Par, as you are outward bound, but I plan to study with Milord Kensington."

"Senior? He's a higher warrior? Bah!"

Mun heaved a sigh. "Par, Milord *Derek* Kensington."

"Derek?" Para's eyes narrowed again as she regarded the warrior. "Why Derek, Munwar?"

"I have been studying to become a Paladin."

Para and her chair toppled backward, heels over head.

The End

About the Author

Nona King has loved writing since she first penned skits and songs as a child. She began writing novels when she was 16 after a friend loaned her older brother an electric typewriter.

For five years starting in 1999, she experimented with writing sci-fi/fantasy stories based in the worlds of role-playing video games. The most popular of those stories was the *Bookworms and Booya!* saga consisting of six novellas following the life of a shy librarian: Sally Regal.

Currently, she is working on finishing book three of her fantasy saga and revising her inspirational romances *Searching for Sara* and *Broken Angel*. She is also planning her entry for the 2009 National Novel Writing month competition. *To Save a Soul* was a winner of the 2008 National Novel Writing month competition.

Nona lives in Kent with her husband Michael, her cat Katie, and their two dogs Eli and Mars.

3489033

Made in the USA